Ethan paused, his voice like the crack of a whip.

"You should add the word 'con' to your job title, Mia! It's the twenty-first century. You can't just pass my brother off as the father because it suits your bank account."

"I'm not trying to *pass* the baby off." Finally she dared look at him. "This is *my* baby, Ethan. In fact, I never intended for you or your family to find out—especially now Richard's…"

"But Richard did die," Ethan said finally. "Richard did die, Mia. And if you're telling the truth, if this is his child, then we've got a helluva lot to talk about!"

She could feel the tiny hairs rising on the back of her neck, the chilling feeling that suddenly everything had become impossibly complicated, and she finally admitted to herself that today wasn't going to bring closure—that things had, in fact, just started.

D1010212

EXPECTING!

She's sexy, successful... and **PREGNANT!**

Relax and enjoy our fabulous series about couples whose passion ends in pregnancies...sometimes unexpected! Of course, the birth of a baby is always a joyful event, and we can guarantee that our characters will become wonderful moms and dads—but what happened in those nine months before?

Share the surprises, emotions, drama and suspense as our parents-to-be come to terms with the prospect of bringing a new baby into the world. All will discover that the business of making babies brings with it the most special love of all....

Delivered only by Harlequin Presents®

Carol Marinelli

HIS PREGNANT MISTRESS

EXPECTING!

HARLEQUIN®

TORONTO • NEW YORK • LONDON
AMSTERDAM • PARIS • SYDNEY • HAMBURG
STOCKHOLM • ATHENS • TOKYO • MILAN • MADRID
PRAGUE • WARSAW • BUDAPEST • AUCKLAND

If you purchased this book without a cover you should be aware that this book is stolen property. It was reported as "unsold and destroyed" to the publisher, and neither the author nor the publisher has received any payment for this "stripped book."

ISBN 0-373-12460-0

HIS PREGNANT MISTRESS

First North American Publication 2005.

Copyright © 2005 by The SAL Marinelli Family Trust.

All rights reserved. Except for use in any review, the reproduction or utilization of this work in whole or in part in any form by any electronic, mechanical or other means, now known or hereafter invented, including xerography, photocopying and recording, or in any information storage or retrieval system, is forbidden without the written permission of the publisher, Harlequin Enterprises Limited, 225 Duncan Mill Road, Don Mills, Ontario, Canada M3B 3K9.

All characters in this book have no existence outside the imagination of the author and have no relation whatsoever to anyone bearing the same name or names. They are not even distantly inspired by any individual known or unknown to the author, and all incidents are pure invention.

This edition published by arrangement with Harlequin Books S.A.

® and TM are trademarks of the publisher. Trademarks indicated with ® are registered in the United States Patent and Trademark Office, the Canadian Trade Marks Office and in other countries.

www.eHarlequin.com

Printed in U.S.A.

CHAPTER ONE

DON'T look up.

Don't look up.

Over and over, Mia said those three little words to herself, knew, without a shadow of a doubt, it was the only way she could get through this dark hour in her life.

She attempted to focus on the order of service she held. Her hands trembled so violently it made reading impossible, which was maybe just as well, for even the photograph of her dear friend Richard smiling back at her was enough to cause a fresh batch of tears to well in her eyes, for the stifled scream to build in her throat at the agonizing end to such a beautiful life; it didn't make sense.

Nothing today made any sense.

Nothing in the formal surrounds of the church, or the austere people that packed the tiny pews, captured the essence of what Richard was about. She could count on one hand Richard's true friends—the so-called dreamers and drifters that were relegated like herself to the back pews of the church. While the Carvelles and their entourage sat at the front, sweltered in the unfamiliar tropical heat in heavy black suits, the sultry, balmy heat of the late afternoon in Cairns clearly a distant memory, as one by one they had drifted down south, as one by one they had abandoned their roots and headed for the concrete security of the financial capital, their money too big, their egos too wide for the lush, unspoilt beauty of far North Queensland where they had first made their fortune, building and developing the type of luxury hotels that ensured the tourists returned. Too much was never enough where the Carvelles were concerned, the grass was always greener, the wallets always deeper somewhere else.

Only Richard had stayed.

As she stared at the order of service her mouth hardened and it took a moment to register that the emotion she was feeling was anger.

Anger towards the insensitive might that was the Carvelles.

Even the photo of him they had chosen looked wrong, wooden and formal in a suit and tie a world away from the casual, scruffy shorts and T-shirt guy Richard was.

Had been.

The mental correction caused a searing pain to rip through her, her hands moving to her stomach, massaging the life within, willing herself to stay calm for the sake of the baby she carried inside.

Richard's baby.

The surge of panic that overwhelmed her was exacerbated by the rustle in the pews as the congregation stood and Mia attempted to stand, her legs trembling violently as the procession moved, willing herself to hold it together, to just get through the necessary formalities without drawing attention to herself.

So she stared down, screwing her eyes closed as the procession passed, the horrible scent of incense from the minister's lantern as he led the mourners an aching reminder of her father's funeral just two years previously. But despite her vow not to look up, to keep to the plan Mia had put in place merely to get her through, as the music stilled, and the congregation hushed, Mia's strategies fell by the wayside as her eyes slowly lifted. Drawn, not to the coffin, but to the dark-suited figure that followed behind, to the face that had haunted her dreams for the last seven years, to the face that had loved her, the eyes that had adored her and to the man who had so cruelly discarded her.

Ethan.

Only his haughty profile was visible as he walked with the sombre procession, taking his place in the front pew, staring fixedly ahead as the minister's voice welcomed the congregation on this sad day.

And though the minister's words were well delivered, though it was Richard that had brought her here today, it was Ethan that held her attention, Ethan whom she stared at as the congregation shuffled to a stand, realizing, not for the first time, just how different Ethan was from his younger brother whom they were here to mourn. Richard, pale-skinned with light auburn hair, so vulnerable and fragile; the absolute antithesis of this confident, jet-haired swarthy-skinned, imposing man standing tall at the front of the church, easily a head above the rest. The only sign of emotion in his impassive face was that his jaw clenched in stony silence as the rest of the congregation started to sing, one hand held behind his back, the knuckles white with tension against his immaculate suit, and as an age-old hymn she'd heard a million times before filled the sacred space only now did she really hear it for the first time, each and every word seeming to dredge through the remnants of her soul. And only now did she really feel it, begin to understand it: the timeless wonder of love, the everlasting promise of peace, and as the words soared skywards, as her tears fell downwards, all Mia could think, all Mia could wish at the loneliest moment of her life was that the man who stood so distant and aloof at the front of the church didn't still touch her so.

She wished with her whole heart that the seven years that had passed since she had seen Ethan Carvelle could have rendered him less impressive, less authoritative…less beautiful.

She had known today would be hard, but it wasn't just saying goodbye to Richard that was on her mind. She had said her farewells to him weeks ago. Expended most of her grief in painful stages as day by day the cancer that had ravaged his body had taken him piece by piece, like a beautiful statue being slowly dismantled, his short-term memory fading first, followed closely by pride as his functions had decreased. Yet all that Mia could deal with, even the agony of watching his sparkling humour slowly slip away, watching as he'd struggled to make a point, to finish a joke, hadn't come close to the tragedy of his vacant eyes, which one black morning, had failed to recognize her. A mouth that hadn't smiled as she'd entered his sun-drenched room in the hospice. Mia had known then that for Richard, her dear, kind Richard, it was over. She had said goodbye to him then, her mourning commencing that very day for the wonderful man who the doctor had gently told her would never now return.

Today was a formality—the end of the tragic end.

She had hoped it would be the same when she saw Ethan.

That seeing him after all this time would bring some closure. That the seven years of pain she had suffered after Ethan's cruel rejection would somehow now abate. That finally after all this time she could really move on with her life.

But watching Ethan as he left his pew and walked towards the front of the church, Mia felt her breath trap in her throat, her legs finally still—cold shock setting in as all over again, as if for the very first time, she witnessed his beauty face on.

He seemed taller if that were possible, his shoulders wider, and the years had treated him kindly. His hair, still jet-black, was cut shorter than it had been seven years ago. The last gasps of the youthful twenty-three-year-old she had witnessed in those unforgettable weeks they had shared were gone for ever now, replaced instead with a savage maturity that quite literally took her breath away. And not just Mia's—the whole church descended into utter silence, every face turned to his commanding figure. Ethan held the packed church in the palm of his hand—not just because he was Richard's brother, not just because his surname happened to be Carvelle, but because the mere sight of him, the very presence of him demanded respect. He could walk into a bar on the other side of the world, order a drink in that measured, clipped voice and every head in the place would turn, every woman would sit up straighter, and every man stand up taller.

He paused before he started his reading, staring down for a fraction of a second. Mia watched his Adam's apple bob up and down, waiting in tense silence as a man used to public speaking prepared himself for the most difficult speech of his life. Seeing the hands that had once tenderly held hers gripping the lectern, proud, tall and commanding as his deep voice delivered the reading, it was as if each word shot an arrow to her already bleeding heart. And it was more than she could bear to watch, sheer torture to see what she could never now have, so she dragged her eyes away from the object of his outer beauty, trying to remember the cruelty within, focusing on her own tightly clasped hands, her fingers interlaced over the soft swell of her stomach, chewing her lip as tears flooded her cheeks, watching as her knees again started to jerk up and down as if dancing to their own private tune as his deep, measured tones ripped through her, every last word the antithesis of the treatment he had dished out to her.

The faith he had shattered, the hope he had destroyed; a fresh batch of tears welled in her eyes as finally the reading turned to what Ethan clearly couldn't give, his voice searing through her as he delivered his final words…

"'Meanwhile these three remain: faith, ho…'" His deep voice wavered and then halted, a tiny cough as he cleared his throat and the beat of a pause dragged on mercilessly, the congregation shuffling uncomfortably as Ethan forced himself to continue.

"'Faith.'" He dragged the single word out, paused a second too long again and Mia found herself mouthing the next word silently to herself, bitterly recalling the hope there had once been, the hope that had surrounded the conception of her child, a future for Richard they had hoped to ensure. But as the pause went on her mind turned again, drifting back along the painful, familiar path she had followed for so long: the road to Ethan. Dragging her eyes up, she recalled the hope that had surrounded them all those years ago, those stolen, balmy weeks when the world seemed to have paused for a while, when they had stood on the threshold of tomorrow, glimpsed a future that might just have been kind, and despite the pain he had caused, despite the agony he had put her and her father through, at that moment she felt for him, felt her heart go out to this strong, proud man as he stood alone at the front of the congregation, for once faltering and hesitant. She felt no joy in watching him suffer, took no pleasure in his pain. His eyes flicked to hers, and for the first time in seven years their eyes met, and it was as if it were just the two of them in the church, as if the years that stretched behind them had somehow melted away and she was in his arms again, the closeness they had once shared somehow captured in that gaze. In an instinctive show of support Mia gave him a tiny nod, told him with her eyes he was doing okay. Like a parent at a school play she willed him to carry on speaking, and it worked, Ethan's eyes holding hers as he finished the reading.

'"Faith, hope and love… And the greatest of these is love."'

Determinedly avoiding her gaze now, he made his way back to his seat, and for Mia the rest of the service passed in a blur. Her tears dried up as finally the crowd moved outside. She took in huge gulps of the humid mid-morning air, blinking at the sunlight as her high heels crunched in the gravel, the congregation slowly working the line, shaking hands with the Carvelles before they headed for the crematorium—a private cremation the order of the day for the Carvelle family. Shutting out friendship, discounting outsiders in their usual closed-rank way; it probably never even entered their heads that in the last few months Mia had spent more time with Richard than the whole lot of them combined.

She could argue the point, if she were that way inclined. Point out that, like it or not, she was very much family now; that the swell of her stomach beneath her black dress meant she had every reason to join them.

But she didn't.

Instead she murmured her condolences, shook hands with the endless faces, and braced herself to kiss the cheeks of Richard's mother as one would for touching a snake. Mia stared into the cold blue eyes of a woman who, though she had borne two sons, didn't have a maternal bone in her body.

'Miss Stewart.' Her lips twisted around the two words, as if it were more than she could bear to say the name.

'I'm sorry for your loss,' Mia responded, willing the line to move, wanting this just to be over with, but Hugh Carvelle was talking intently to another dark-suited gentleman and, Mia realized with a sinking feeling, she'd have to face Richard's mother for a little while longer yet.

'It's a blessing,' Rosalind said in a practised voice, 'Richard was in a lot of pain.'

And maybe the polite thing would have been to murmur her understanding, but quite simply Mia couldn't do it. What would this woman know about Richard's pain? How did she even have the gall to comment when, despite Mia's phone calls urging her to come, she'd barely spent an hour with her son over the last few weeks, waltzing into the hospice for a brief visit before disappearing again? And where was the blessing?

Where was the blessing when a twenty-eight-year-old man lay dead?

Taking a deep breath, Mia willed herself calm, choked back the fury that welled inside her, told herself that Rosalind Carvelle was a grieving mother, that it wasn't for Mia to judge, then let out a long sigh of relief when finally the line moved on. Mia listened as Hugh, clearly not even recognizing her, not even remembering that it had been her father he had so cruelly dismissed from his employment seven years ago, invited her back to a five star hotel for a dignified drink after the private cremation. Mia willed the line to move faster, despite the open space positively claustrophobic now as the moment she simultaneously dreaded and yearned for drew nearer, her breath so shallow she could barely catch it as finally Ethan's hand closed around hers. She didn't need to look up to know it was his, felt the force of his presence as they stood just a few inches apart, the touch of his skin on her hand enough to trigger a response only Ethan could ever yield.

'Mia.' His voice was low; she could feel his eyes burning into the top of her head as she stared fixedly at the ground. 'Thank you for coming today. I know it would have meant a lot to Richard.'

'How?' Glittering eyes snapped up to his. 'How do you know that it would have meant a lot to Richard when you barely even spoke to him?'

And she hadn't wanted to do this, hadn't wanted any sort of confrontation, had merely hoped just to make it through, so why was she courting disaster now? Why was she staring defiantly into the face of the man who had, not only cruelly broken her heart, but dragged her unsuspecting father into things just to turn the knife a touch further? Why wasn't she walking away with the last shred of dignity she had instead of exposing her pain? Instead of staring at that unscrupulous face and questioning his love for his brother?

He couldn't look.

Couldn't look into those two sparkling jewels that always dragged him in, those aquamarine pools that had once captured his heart, remembering in that instant the first time they had met, how she had, quite simply, ensnared him with a smile.

Even before the waitress had led him to the table outside on the balcony, as he'd walked through the massive glassed doors his eyes had darted to where she'd sat. Her bronzed skin glistening in the low evening sun; eyes mirrored by glasses as she'd stared out onto the ocean; a soft mint-coloured linen shift dress that showed a tantalizing glimpse of toned slender thighs; simple silver sandals on her feet. Every detail Ethan had processed in a second, except her hair—blonde, tumbling ringlets piled loosely on top of her head—had taken a few seconds longer. So had the long, slender neck, long silver earrings dancing in the seductive shadow of her throat even though her head had been perfectly still. Even if the waitress had led him to another table, Ethan would, quite simply, have had to go over, to introduce himself to this incredible parcel of femininity. But in a delicious twist of fate the waitress had been leading him to her table.

'Mia Stewart.' She smiled as he sat down, held out a slender hand as he forcefully reminded himself that tonight was strictly business.

Business, Ethan reminded himself, forcing himself to get a grip. Richard was missing and this lady surely knew why.

Every road in his investigations had led him to her.

Mia Stewart—Richard's hippy, arty girlfriend.

Mia Stewart—daughter of the manager of the Cairns Hotel. The manager who was secretly being investigated. Some of his transactions had caught Ethan's sharp eye in the Sydney office and he had alerted his father. Any day now, Conner Stewart would be marched out of the office, not only without a golden handshake, but, if Ethan's suspicions were confirmed, his wrist would be encased, not with a heavy watch to mark his years of service, but with handcuffs.

'I'm Ethan.' Offering his hand, somehow he kept his voice even, managed his usual detached smile as her hand met his, the other pulling down her sunglasses. 'Thank you for agreeing to see me.'

'How could I not?' She gave a small shrug. 'It all sounds very mysterious. Richard's disappeared and you assume I know his whereabouts. You've got me intrigued.'

'I'm the one who's intrigued,' Ethan replied evenly. 'You're supposed to be his girlfriend, yet you've no idea as to his whereabouts.'

'You've got it all wrong.'

'I don't think so…' Ethan started, but his voice trailed off as Mia carried on talking.

'You see, Richard and I are just friends.'

Normally he would have pushed further, questioned

her harder, but her glasses were off now, revealing aquamarine eyes, thickly framed with dark lashes, eyes as deep and as divine as the ocean that glittered behind, as entrancing and as captivating as the woman who was staring back now, and Ethan beat back the first blush that had graced his cheeks in a decade.

Mia Stewart, who that very moment had captured his heart...

'I know that you and Richard were close.' His hand was still holding hers, black eyes still boring into the top of her head, his voice steady, not a trace of the hesitancy that had stilled him in the church. 'I know that the last few weeks must have been a terrible strain and that today must be hard for you too.' His eyes dragged down and she could feel the blood rushing to her pale cheeks, colour suffusing her, her heart rate quickening more if that were possible as the weight of his gaze dusted her body. Her breath held hot in her bursting lungs as he took in the ripe swell of her stomach beneath her black linen dress, and she could feel the scorching heat from those black coal chips as they flicked down to her hands, undoubtedly taking in the absence of a ring. 'Will you and your partner be joining the family for a drink after the cremation?'

'I'm here alone.'

He nodded, those dark eyes giving nothing away. He might just as well have been wearing shades for all the expression in his eyes as he stared directly back at her.

'Perhaps we could talk...'

'I really don't think there's much to talk about, do you?'

'I meant about Richard.' For the first time he looked uncomfortable but he quickly recovered. 'Wakes are supposed to be important for grieving, for remembering...'

'I'll remember Richard in my own way,' Mia broke in. 'And I certainly don't need the Carvelles to give me permission to grieve.'

The fire died in Mia then. She couldn't do this, couldn't stand and score points off Ethan Carvelle, couldn't besmirch Richard's memory in this way, yet neither could she pretend to give or receive comfort to his cold, self-serving family, on this, one of the blackest days of her life.

It was safer to leave now.

Reclaiming her hand, she made her way down the line, holding her tears, her grief firmly back, her hand still tingling from his touch, the one area of warmth in her cold, frozen body apart from the silent tears that trickled down her now pale cheeks.

And she held it in, held it deep inside, watching in respectful silence as the coffin was loaded into the hearse, Ethan, proud and tall, carrying his brother on his broad shoulders for his final journey, a flash of tears in those black eyes, that delicious mouth quilted in pain.

Only when the entourage departed did her emotions finally catch up.

Only as she watched the car containing Richard disappear out of sight, the back of Ethan's head in the family car following slowly behind, did the true depth of her loss finally hit Mia.

Her hands gripping her stomach, she contemplated the baby inside, the father it would now never meet, the loving gesture that had seemed so right at the time, so straightforward and uncomplicated, terrifying her now, spinning her into a panic that would surely never end. The full weight of responsibility descending on her tired shoulders seemed almost too much to bear.

Silver spots danced before Mia's eyes; as the floor seemed to spin around her she could hear the worried shouts from the crowd as they dashed over, see the floor coming to meet her as she sank down onto the grass.

Grief, agony, both past and present all homing in, all suffocating her with the impossibility of her situation. But it wasn't that her baby's father was dead, wasn't that she was in this alone now that seemed to be smothering her as she struggled merely to breathe.

Worse, far worse than her loss was the knowledge she had gained today. As much as she hated him, as much as every fibre of her being loathed him for all he had put her and her father through, seeing Ethan again, feeling his hand on hers, listening to that deep, measured voice, staring for that moment into his dark brooding eyes, Mia realized it was for ever. Knew that after all these years the feelings were still as strong, the pain he had inflicted was everlasting, the closure she craved would never eventuate, the grief that gripped her now, had suffused her for seven years, would never, ever relent.

She could hear the ambulance sirens, was vaguely aware of a mask being slipped over her face, the cool, dark confines of the ambulance as they closed the doors and pulled away from the church towards the hospital.

But none of it mattered, none of it registered, not when a life of agony stretched before her.

She still loved Ethan Carvelle.

CHAPTER TWO

'WE'D really rather keep you in.' A rather impatient-looking doctor stared at her notes. 'At least for a couple of days until your blood pressure comes down.'

'It's hardly likely to come down here,' Mia replied through gritted teeth, wishing they would all just leave her alone, that she could get in her car and drive back to her home to pore over the day's events in her own surrounds. 'Once I'm home I'll be fine.'

'What if you're not?' The doctor stared at her coolly over his glasses. 'You don't live locally, Ms Stewart; you live two hours out of Cairns in the mountains. It's all very well for you to take risks with your own health, but bear in mind that you're seven months pregnant. Arguing over a couple of days' admission…'

'Who's arguing?'

Thank God they'd taken the blood-pressure machine off her arm, because if her reading had been high before, as Ethan's dry tones filled the rather small cubicle Mia was sure it would be up through the roof about now. His heavy cologne mingled with the sickly antiseptic smell, his height, his presence dwarfing everything, and even the rather terse doctor seemed to take on rather more courteous tones as he addressed Ethan.

'I was just explaining to your wife, sir—'

'She's not my wife,' Ethan corrected, totally at ease as the doctor's eyes swivelled nervously to the notes in his hands.

'Well, your partner, then. I was trying to explain that it's imperative she stay in hospital for a couple of days for the baby's sake...'

'She's not my partner either,' Ethan said with a slight edge. 'She's a *friend*.'

'I'm most certainly not!' Mia retorted. 'A passing acquaintance would be a more apt description.'

'Prickly, isn't she?' Ethan smiled and if the doctor wasn't already gay he was certainly heading for conversion because he practically melted on the spot as Ethan turned his black eyes to him. 'What exactly is the problem, Doctor?'

Mia's horrified expression at Ethan's rude intrusion should have been enough to stop the doctor in his tracks, but given both men's backs were practically to her she lay instead welling with indignation as they proceeded to discuss her as if she weren't in the room.

'Her blood pressure's high and according to her blood work she was slightly dehydrated when she arrived as well as underweight. We just want to keep her here for a couple of days to make sure everything's progressing normally with the pregnancy.'

Mia was about to respond but held back when Ethan's calm, measured tones appeared to support what she'd been saying.

'What if she agreed to come back tomorrow for a

check-up? Surely her own home would be the best place for her to rest?'

'Normally, yes, but given she lives a two-hour drive away it's out of the question. She needs to be resting, not driving a car along winding mountain roads, and if something goes wrong help isn't easily at hand.'

'Fair enough.' Ethan nodded. 'Don't worry, Doctor, I'll soon talk her around.'

'You will not!'

Remembering, finally, that Mia was actually the patient, the doctor actually managed to address her. 'I'm waiting for your GP to call through with your antenatal history, but in the meantime I want you to lie there and relax, and perhaps your "passing acquaintance" might be able to talk some sense into you.'

'I'll do my best!'

Alone with Ethan the fire seemed to die within her. Impossibly shy and confused, she stared again at her fingers, utterly refusing to look up, to be the one to break the oppressive silence, but, when it was clear Ethan had more staying power than her, finally Mia relented.

'What are you doing here?'

'I'm beginning to wonder,' Ethan quipped. 'I should be halfway down a bottle of whisky by now and regaling tales of Richard's and my supposedly happy childhood...' His voice trailed off and if she'd looked up she'd have seen his face soften slightly. 'When I got back to the hotel I heard a woman had collapsed at the funeral. The words ''blonde'' and ''pregnant'' kind of narrowed the field.'

'You didn't need to come.'

'I know,' he admitted, 'but I was worried about you.'

'It's a bit late to be worried about me, Ethan!' She could hear the bitterness in her own voice. 'Seven years too late, actually. You lost all right to worry about me when you walked, or rather flew, out on me without a backwards glance. You lost all right to worry about me when you arranged to have my father sacked two days later…'

'He wasn't sacked,' Ethan retorted. 'I distinctly remember signing the cheque—'

'He was sacked!' Mia broke in, her voice choking with emotion at the memory of her father's strained face, the utter devastation as he'd slumped in his chair that afternoon, told Mia that after twenty years of devoted service the Carvelles had accused him of theft. 'And worse, he was expected to be grateful that you hadn't called the police…'

'He was fiddling the books, Mia…' Ethan's voice was pure ice, his stance unequivocal, but seeing her lie back on the pillow, the swell of her stomach beneath the white sheet, witnessing firsthand the utter exhaustion and devastation on her proud face as she lay struggling to hold it together, he chose to relent.

'I just wanted to make sure you were okay.'

'Which I am.'

'Not according to the doctor,' Ethan pointed out,

but his voice was gentler now. 'He seems to think that you're not well at all.'

'This isn't your problem.'

'I know.'

'In fact…' Mia's voice gave an involuntary wobble but she quickly recovered '…this has absolutely nothing to do with you.'

'Thank God,' Ethan muttered, flashing a malevolent smile, just to show he was still in control. 'So I take it you want me to go?'

Mia nodded, not trusting herself to speak. Ethan leaving was the last thing she wanted, but it was safer, so very much safer this way.

'I'll let the rest of your visitors in on my way out, shall I?'

'The rest of my visitors?' She stared at him nonplussed, simultaneously kicking herself as she realized she'd fallen directly into his trap.

'I thought as much,' Ethan said with a note of triumph. 'There's not exactly a queue of concerned visitors outside, waiting to drive you home. What about the baby's father?'

She could feel the sweat beading on her forehead, feel its icy rivers trickling between her breasts, her pale cheeks flushing as Ethan's eyes bored into her, running a tongue over impossibly dry lips as she carefully chose her words.

'He's not in the picture any more.'

His breath hissed out, the longest silence followed by the sharpest of words. 'Another ''passing acquaintance'', I presume.'

'Much more than that.' She stared at him, eyes glittering in pain, honesty a breath away but she held it in.

'So tell me, Mia, are you planning to drive yourself home?'

'Of course. I'm fine!''

'Not according to this you're not.' Picking up her chart, he skimmed his eyes down it; not like a normal person, though, Mia noted. Normal people squinted at charts upside down, made sure no one was looking as they tried to decipher what had been written, but Ethan Carvelle, damn him, was holding the chart and reading it authoritatively as if he were the blessed consultant. 'It says here that you're underweight, dehydrated and your blood pressure's way too high.'

'Of course it's high.' Mia's voice was rising now. 'I've spent the last few months driving up and down the mountains every day to visit Richard as well as trying to keep the gallery going…'

'Gallery?'

'My old studio. The one my father…'

'The one where we…' His voice trailed off as he apparently realised the danger in pursuing that line of questioning. The fact they had first made love there had no bearing on today. Could never have any bearing now.

'It's a gallery now,' Mia said instead for him. 'And the reason my blood pressure is up is because, not only have I been neglecting it of late, not only am I way behind with some paintings I've been commissioned to do, I've also just lost my best friend in the whole world…' her voice wobbled, the tiniest, most irrelevant of problems surfacing now, an attempt perhaps to drag her mind away from the true preposterousness of her situation '…and to top it all I'm on a two-hour park in the middle of the city…'

Tears started then, horrible, uninvited tears that she didn't want him to witness, that she didn't want to stoop to, but, seeing him there, another layer of emotion on top of her hellish day was all too much and the tension, the utter, unbearable tension that had been holding her together, snapped then, whipping her reserve away as sobs drenched her fatigued body. Ethan was over in a second, pulling her into his arms and holding her tightly. It was the only place on earth she wanted to be, the only place she had ever truly belonged. And even though it was wrong, even though it could surely only complicate things, right here, right now she needed him. She wanted those strong arms to hold her and needed just a fraction of the strength that was Ethan Carvelle. Even though it was only transitory, and for all the wrong reasons, she allowed herself the indulgence of being held by him, of just letting go and leaning on him for a tiny while.

'I don't pretend to know a thing about art—' his voice was low and deep and comforting '—and I know I don't mean a thing to you compared to Richard…' She inhaled his scent, dragged on his strength, even moved her head a fraction in denial. Nothing could ever replace Richard, but Ethan was *everything* to her, always had been, and always would be, but sensibility prevailed, holding her back at the final moment, keeping in what could never, ever be said. 'But if a car needs moving, then I'm your man.'

The flash of humour was so unforeseen, so unexpected, it toppled her over the edge. Clinging on for dear life, she found herself letting go, really letting go, perhaps for the first time in seven years.

'Let it out, Mia.' His face was buried in her hair, her cheek against his chest feeling every breath he took as his heart hammered against her. His elusive scent she had chased for seven years filled her nostrils, and he was all she needed, everything she needed and maybe, just maybe, now she could tell him.

'Ms Stewart?' The doctor was back, an unwelcome intrusion, and Mia stiffened, but still Ethan held her…still she clung on. 'I've just spoken to your GP on the telephone; he's filled me in a bit on your history. I'm very sorry—I didn't realize that it was the baby's father you buried today…'

Mia felt Ethan tense in her arms. His breathing stilled for an impossibly long time, then tripped into overdrive as he broke away. But as he lay her back on the pillow not a flicker of his expression relayed his reaction to the news as her anguished eyes searched his. 'Perhaps given the circumstances…' the doctor droned on, utterly oblivious to the bombshell he had just dropped, impervious to the mounting tension in the room '…home might be the best place for you. I'd prefer if we let the drip finish, though, so we can ensure that you're adequately rehydrated, and I

want you back here tomorrow or at your local GP's
to have that blood pressure checked.'

'Thank you,' Mia croaked, dreading what she
might see, yet looking for some type of reaction, trying to fathom Ethan's take on the news he had just
heard, but his expression gave away nothing.

'Naturally, someone should drive you home.'

'I will.' Ethan's voice was supremely calm. 'How
long till the drip finishes?'

'An hour or so,' the doctor answered.

'Give me your keys.' Rummaging under the trolley, he pulled out her handbag and tossed it beside
her. 'I'll go and fetch your car for you.' He shot her
a black look. 'At least it will be one less thing for
you to worry about.'

'But you don't know which one it is,' Mia answered, flustered, but Ethan didn't deign a response,
just took the keys without another word to her, saving
all his icy venom for the poor doctor.

'I'll be back within the hour, Doctor. And for the
record, Ms Stewart is grief-stricken, she's clearly in
no fit state to discharge herself, so I strongly suggest
that if she isn't here when I return you've made damn
sure your medical indemnity insurance is fully paid
up.'

The doctor was no match for Ethan's stern glare
and scuttled gratefully out. Ethan stood, silently staring—and suddenly Mia didn't want Ethan's take on
this, didn't want to hear his reaction to the news that
had just been imparted. Pleating the sheet between her
fingers, she stared down, feeling the anger, the incre-

dulity emanating from Ethan, could feel the disdain blazing from his eyes even though she couldn't bring herself to look at them.

'Sweet little Mia,' he said finally, his voice like the crack of a whip. 'You should add the word "con" to your job title, Mia! Well, you might be able to fool the doctors, your friends, hell, even a few journalists into believing your half-baked story, but it's the twenty-first century, Mia. You can't just pass Richard off as the father because it suits your bank account.'

'I'm not trying to *pass* the baby off.' Finally she dared look at him. 'This is *my* baby, Ethan. In fact, I never intended for you or your family to find out. It was you who came here, remember; you who chose to ride roughshod and stand over me while the doctor was here.'

'Bull.' His voice was menacingly quiet, his head slowly shaking in sheer disbelief. 'If this is Richard's baby, how come we don't know? Why on earth wouldn't he tell us?' When she didn't answer he pressed on relentlessly. 'If this is my brother's child, why aren't there provisions for it in his will?'

'Because there wasn't time, and, as much as I didn't want you to know, I'm not going to deny Richard now. I'm not going to pretend it's not his child just to make you feel better. But for your information I was always going to raise this baby alone; it was how we planned it!'

'What?' Incredulous eyes snapped to hers.

'I was going to bring up the baby alone, whatever

happened to Richard. I always intended to be the sole carer...'

'Who needs a man in their life?' he jeered. 'What the hell's the point of rotting up a kid with a male perspective on life? Is this one of your half-baked hippy schemes that you roped Richard into, Mia? One of the trendy bandwagons you decided to jump on board...' He shook his head. 'You don't fool me for a moment, Mia Stewart. You had this planned down to the last detail, didn't you? This was your last little stab at the Carvelle fortune.' She opened her mouth to argue but he overrode her in an instant. 'Well, bring it on, Mia.' The hands that beckoned her were anything but welcoming, his unusually pale face savage in the fluorescent hospital light. 'Bring it on, because I'm ready for you—more ready than you'll ever know.'

'What's that supposed to mean?' In an instinctive gesture her hands cradled her stomach, pulling her knees up, protecting the one thing on God's earth that was hers and hers alone. 'You don't scare me, Ethan, and as hard as it may be for you to believe your wealth doesn't intimidate me either. I don't want a cent from the Carvelles.' She let out a low, mirthless laugh. 'I don't want them anywhere near me, in fact, but I will not deny this child its father. I will not lie here and tell you it's not Richard's child just to make things easier for me. This *is* Richard's baby and I'll never be ashamed of that fact.'

Something in her voice seemed to reach him, something in the proud jut of her chin, the glittering anger in her eyes halted his angry retort. His eyes drifted down to her stomach, staring at the firm mound under the sheet, one hand moving to his face, covering his mouth for a second. Then he closed his eyes and for an appalling moment she thought he was going to break down, that the impervious mask that was Ethan Carvelle was about to slip, but he recovered quickly, dragging his eyes back to her, repeating a question that she still hadn't answered, but from the hoarseness in his voice, the slight grey tinge creeping into his features, Mia knew his world had been rocked, knew he was actually starting to believe that the baby she was carrying might be Richard's.

'Why didn't we know?' His voice was raw and he cleared his throat, fixing her with his black stare, but it wasn't quite so assured now. 'If what you're saying is true, why the hell didn't Richard say anything? He never even implied you were anything more than friends...'

'During one of your weekly phone calls?' Mia retorted nastily, but she was beyond caring now, the implication that she was in this only for the money too abhorrent not to reciprocate with harsh words of her own. 'Or perhaps he should have included it in one of the regular emails you fired to each other...' Seeing the pain in his eyes, she realized she'd gone too far; the day of Richard's funeral was hardly the time to point out the void between them, the tragedy of a relationship reduced to stilted birthday and Christmas cards. And, Mia thought reluctantly, given the rapidly unfolding circumstances, given the

Carvelle name and all its implications, Ethan's reaction was probably merited.

It wasn't his fault that she loved him.

'I'm sorry, that was uncalled for.' After the longest pause she found her voice.

'It's the truth.' Ethan shrugged.

'But this really was a very much wanted baby.'

Maybe Mia's gloves were off, but Ethan's were still firmly tied on, every word a painful punch to her already fragile soul.

'Please.' His voice was dripping with sarcasm as he hit her while she was down. 'So wanted that none of his family even knew about it, so wanted we didn't even know he was dating you, so wanted that a baby wasn't even on the agenda till he was dying…'

'He wasn't supposed to die!' Agony rasped in every word, her strained voice overriding his powerful one on emotion alone, forcing a quiet, forcing him to stop his tirade to stand stock-still as Mia continued. 'He wasn't supposed to die,' she said again, but Ethan remained unmoved.

'He had cancer, Mia. The doctors gave him eighteen months, two years at most. So what the hell was he doing having children? What the hell was he doing bringing a child into the world he would surely never be there to watch grow up? It just doesn't add up.'

'We don't all live by your rules, Ethan; we don't all walk around with a mental calculator weighing up the pros and cons, checking for longevity and distant projections. Richard knew he might never see his child grow up and I knew it too, but it was a risk we were prepared to take…'

'You really talked about it?' His voice told her the preposterousness he felt in her actions. The incredulity in his eyes as he stared back at her only distanced him further, yet she ached to reach him, to drag him beside her, to reach an understanding while somehow avoiding the truth.

'We talked about it for weeks, Ethan, for weeks.'

'So it wasn't an accident, a one-night stand…'

'This was a wanted baby, Ethan.'

'Oh, I bet it was,' Ethan hissed. 'It's what you've been wanting for years, isn't it, Mia?'

'Ethan, please, you don't understand…'

'Don't I?' Ethan snapped, his face menacingly close as the doctor melted away. 'Save the tears, Mia. You've got what you wanted, or most of it.'

'Meaning?'

'You couldn't quite manage to hook the Carvelle surname for yourself, but you'd use a dying, confused man to ensure you snaked your way in somehow. But you've picked the wrong family, Mia. If you think for one second my parents are going to be the pushover Richard clearly was, then I'm about to burst your bubble, darling…' His lips sneered around the word, no sentiment intended as he spat the endearment. 'They'll wrap you up so tightly in legal red tape you'll be pulling your pension before you see a single cent for your efforts.'

'You bastard.'

'No.' Ethan shook his head, his eyes glittering with

rage, his face taut, his breath hot on her cheeks, his hand moving to her stomach and holding the swollen flesh for a moment, shuttering his eyes for a second as if it physically hurt to touch her, to feel the life within her. 'That's what this little one is; that's the level you'd stoop to, to get what you want.'

'This was never about money.'

'Good,' Ethan quipped, 'because you'll die waiting before my parents come around. No smiling, cooing baby will melt their cold hearts.'

'I don't need the Carvelles' money,' Mia hissed. 'I have a life, a home, a career I'm proud of and I'll do just fine on my own.'

She thought that was the end of it, almost thought she'd seen the last of him, that Ethan would walk off now, but still he stood, his eyes narrowing as he stared down at her.

'So what now?'

'You get on with your life and I'll get on with mine,' Mia snapped, but even as the words came out she sensed their futility, knew that now Ethan knew it was Richard's child she was carrying he couldn't just walk away. 'I don't expect you to understand, Ethan,' she said more softly. 'I don't expect you to understand what Richard and I shared, but all I ask is that you believe me when I say that this had nothing to do with money and everything to do with love. He wasn't supposed to die…' Tears brimmed in those aquamarine pools, and the colour was so vivid, so reminiscent of the beautiful land she inhabited, for a tiny second there he felt as if he had come home.

Home, not just to the tropical paradise of Cairns, where lush green trees reached for a sky that blended with the ocean, but home to the capricious, captivating spirit of Mia, and so alien was the feeling that welled inside him, so physical the pain that suddenly gripped him, it took a second for Ethan to register it as need. A need so pure he could feel it, a yearning almost for the balmy, safe haven he had found all those years ago, for the time spent in each other's arms and minds, when the world had seemed at peace, when there was nothing he wouldn't have done for her; and he ached, ached to reach over to catch the splash of tears that rolled down her cheeks, to pull her in his arms and make her world safe.

But he couldn't.

Couldn't allow himself to fall under her spell again, couldn't go through it again and expect to come out the other side. He had to be strong here, had to remain impervious to her charms, hold onto his head and forget about his heart.

'But he did die,' Ethan said finally. 'Richard did die, Mia, and if you're telling the truth, if this is his child, then we've got a hell of a lot to talk about!'

She could feel the tiny hairs rising on the back of her neck, the chilling feeling that suddenly everything had become impossibly complicated, finally admitted to herself that today wasn't going to bring closure, that things had, in fact, just started.

'Wait here,' he ordered, jangling her car keys in his pocket and pinning her with his eyes. 'I'll go and get your car, but don't even think about discharging yourself and jumping in a taxi, Mia. Believe me, I'll find you.'

CHAPTER THREE

SHE should go.

Every sensible thought told Mia to just demand the drip be taken down, pack up her few things, jump in a taxi and get the hell out of there.

Ethan Carvelle had no say here. He couldn't demand she stay at the hospital; he had nothing to do with this.

Time and again she pushed down the cot side of the trolley, picked up a cotton swab, ready to pull the blessed drip out herself. It was her life, her choice if she walked out of the hospital this very moment; his idle threats bore no weight in the real world. Ethan Carvelle counted for nothing here.

But time and again she pulled the side of the trolley back up, leant against the pillows in utter defeat as the fluid dripped into her veins, knowing it was only herself she was kidding.

Ethan Carvelle counted for *everything*.

He had since that day seven long, lonely years ago when he had walked into that restaurant. Every pore, every inch of her skin had screamed for him since then, since that one sweet moment when he had not only taken her virginity, but altered her whole perspective, shifted the lens, made the world sharper

37

somehow, invigorated her, exhausted her, engulf-ed her.

And maybe she could leave now, could get up and walk away, but the action would be merely physical. Her mind, her soul, her heart were constantly with him and she begged for resolution, needed this chance of closure as much as Ethan clearly did.

Needed to tell him how much he had hurt her, needed this time together before she closed this pain-ful chapter for good and moved on.

And it had to be closed, Mia reminded herself; there was too much water under the bridge for any-thing else.

She sensed his presence before she saw him.

Felt the tension in the room lift a notch as the doc-tor removed her drip and the nurse helped her out of her gown, and tried to ply her shaking body into the beastly black dress.

'I'll take it from here.'

He stood at the entrance to the cubicle, supremely in control, trapping her with his gaze as the medical personnel drifted off.

'I can dress myself, thank you.'

But pride had no place in this cramped hospital cubicle; shaking hands and his unwavering gaze made the simplest task impossible. With only one stocking on it was easier to rip it off than attempt the other, forcing bare feet into way-too-high heels, then reluc-tantly taking his hand as she lowered herself off the trolley.

'Have you got everything?'

'Apart from my pride.' Angry eyes met his. 'How dare you demand I stay till you return? How dare you exert your authority on the hospital staff and talk about me as if I were some sort of unhinged person? I nearly went, you know.'

'But you didn't,' Ethan pointed out, not remotely fazed by her outburst. 'Turn around; your zip's undone.'

And if she hadn't been seven months pregnant she'd have reached her hand behind her back and pulled it up herself in one lithe movement, but pregnancy allowed for no such luxuries, and pulling her dress to her waist and half doing the blessed zip up then twisting it around as she had done this morning clearly wasn't an option right now. Instead, burning with shame, she stood stock still, refusing his order to turn around, her breath catching in her throat when Ethan gave an easy shrug and moved behind her, piling her blonde curls unceremoniously on top of her head and lifting her hand to hold them.

'It's stuck.' She could feel his breath on her neck, feel his warm fingers as they tugged at the treacherous zipper that had chosen the worst possible time to give in on her. Okay, it wasn't a maternity dress, just a simple linen shift, and maybe Mia had been pushing her luck choosing to wear it today, but never had she envisaged this outcome. When she had put it on this morning, not for a single second had it entered her head that Ethan Carvelle would be dressing her later.

Undressing her maybe.

The honest admission, even if it was only to her-self, caused a deep blush to darken her cheeks, spreading over her neck and down to her swollen breasts. As his hands made contact with her spine it was as if he'd reached into her body and touched her somewhere deep inside, her whole body involuntarily quivering as slowly he worked the zip upwards, press-ing one hand onto her exposed flesh, past the black of her bra strap, up between her shoulder blades, her arms trembling as she held her hair out of the way, eyes closing as he moved to the tiny hook and eye at the top of the neckline, his touch more than she could bear and be expected to breathe.

'That's fine.' Pulling away too sharply, she shook her head slightly, his bland, utterly unmoved expres-sion only serving to exacerbate her palpable tension. 'Can I go home now?'

'Of course.'

'You collected my car?' Mia checked and Ethan nodded. 'How did you know which one it was?' Her eyes narrowed, watching every flicker of his reaction, waiting for a blush, a look of discomfort to flash over his face, but Ethan remained unmoved, giving a small shrug before he answered.

'I've been watching you.'

'Watching me?' Appalled by his answer, gibbering with rage, she stepped closer, but instead of stepping back Ethan stood his ground, the closeness she had instigated excruciatingly uncomfortable for Mia, but having zero effect on Ethan as her enraged voice rose.

'What do you mean you've been watching me? For how long?'

'A few weeks now.' Ethan shrugged. 'Despite your little speech about being the only one close to Richard, Mia, the simple fact is that I've visited my brother regularly. Towards the end I visited him every day, in fact.'

'But you live in Sydney, your whole family's in Sydney now…'

'Correct. And as much as you'd like to write us all off and give more weight to your theory that all Carvelles are callous, the simple fact of the matter is that since Richard was diagnosed as terminal I flew to Cairns every week to visit him, which is no small journey, and towards the end, when I knew time was running out, I moved into one of my properties here so I could spend more time with him.'

It was too much to take in. Her mind whirred, reeling at the information, that Ethan had been here, that he had been watching her these past few weeks, had been in the hospice holding Richard's hand. Mia's mouth opened and closed over and over, hundreds of questions bobbing on her tongue as she tried to fathom what exactly it was she wanted to ask.

Ethan answered her unvoiced question.

'I avoided you, Mia.' His words were short and clipped, his eyes more menacing than she could ever have imagined, unrecognizable from the giving young man who had made love to her all those years ago, a world away from the tenderness he had once so easily imparted. 'Truth be known, I could think of nothing worse than being in the same room as you: a confrontation at a dying man's bedside really isn't my style. Despite the crap you might have read about me, I do have some standards.'

'No, Ethan, you don't.' It was Mia's voice that was short now, Mia's voice unwavering and in control, her eyes defiant as she stared back at him. 'I've read all about your multimillion-dollar deals, circling like a vulture over failing hotel businesses then swooping in and buying them for a song.'

'That's business.' Ethan shrugged.

'Perhaps,' Mia conceded, but her stance stayed strong. 'But what about the women, Ethan? What about the women you woo into your bed, only to discard the following morning?'

'I'm not into one-night stands,' Ethan clipped. 'If you actually read the papers a bit more closely you'd have realized most of my relationships survive a bit longer than that.'

'Not much,' Mia sneered. 'A week, a month at the most.'

'So?' Ethan shrugged. 'I don't lie, Mia. I never promise it's going to be for ever, and if you actually asked any of the women I've dated in the past I can guarantee not one of them regret it, however short and sweet it may have been.'

'You can guarantee it, can you?' Her lips were set in a taut line, her breasts rising and falling as if they had a life of their own as the unleashed fury that had held her together for seven years ripped out of control. 'Well, here's one woman that regrets it, Ethan.

You're now looking at a woman who wishes more than ever that she hadn't been one of your ships that passed in the night, who would love to turn back the clock and wipe out every last piece of memory of the time we shared.'

'Liar.' One finger slowly razored her cheek, working its way past her ear, down the hollows of her neck till it met the flickering pulse in her neck. Transfixed, filled with loathing and lust, she stared back at him, stared back at the man who seemed to read her innermost thoughts, the man whom she had physically pushed aside in every waking moment but who had, for seven long years, slipped into her dreams every long, lonely night. She wished she could lie better, wished she could stare back and tell him that she meant every word she had said, but her mouth wouldn't move, she couldn't force her lips around the words as relentlessly he continued. 'You *live* to remember it, Mia. I was there, remember; I felt you writhing in my arms, heard you calling out my name, so don't stand there and tell me you wish it had never happened. Don't try and pretend I'm not the best damn lover you ever had…'

'Is everything okay?' The doctor was back, staring nervously at the two of them, and Mia wrestled to stay calm, certain that if they took her blood pressure now there was no way on earth they'd let her out.

'Everything's fine,' Ethan said coolly, picking up her frozen hand and wrapping it possessively in his. 'In fact, I'm just about to take Ms Stewart home.'

*   *   *

The cool night air on her flaming cheeks was bliss, a gentle breeze around her bare legs as she clipped along beside him, feeling the sizzling hatred emanating from her. Even though she was confused, and though the day had spun irretrievably out of control, there was some solace to be had from being with Ethan now.

That finally after all these years she had faced him.

Stood up to him even.

And maybe, maybe an end to her agony was in sight, when whatever had to be said was finally over, when questions that had hung in the air had actually been answered, she could finally walk away.

Emotionally bruised perhaps.

Still loving him, probably.

But seven years of being left in the dark, of never fully understanding why, with no explanation, he had walked away from all they'd had, had drained every last vestige of inner reserve. Surely the truth, however unpalatable, however much it cheapened their time together, was better than the darkness through which she had stumbled these past years.

She would let him drive her home, Mia had already decided on that. The two-hour drive was surely enough time to glean the answers she craved, and then she'd call him a taxi.

Ethan Carvelle could afford it!

'Where's my car?' Staring at the luxury sports model bleeping as the doors unlocked, Mia shook her head. 'You said you'd collect my car.'

'Which I did.' Ethan shrugged.

'So where is it?'

'Scaring the neighbours in my driveway,' he responded easily. 'You didn't think I was going to let you drive home, after what the doctor said?'

'Of course not. I thought that *you* were taking me home.'

'Which I am,' Ethan clipped.

'I mean *my* home…' her voice trailed off as Ethan let out a mirthless laugh.

'What? You really thought I was going to take you to your little love shack in the hills? Sorry, darling, I'm simply not up to a two-hour drive. I, for one, need a stiff drink and a marble bathroom with hot running water, none of which, I'm quite sure, you can provide.' He held up a hand to halt her tirade. 'Elderberry wine and tepid, solar-heated water really aren't my thing…' Staring hard at her, his eyes narrowed, his lips set in such grim determination Mia knew that any argument would be wasted, that Ethan had long ago made up his mind about her and the life she led. 'Let's get one thing straight, Mia. You can risk your own health, hell, once this baby's born you can jump out of a plane without a parachute for all I care, but if you think for one moment that I'm going to let you head off to the mountains to lead your so-called bohemian lifestyle while you wait for the inheritance to flood in, then you've got another think coming. This child deserves a damn sight more than you can give and I'm going to make damn sure it gets it. Now get in the car!'

Despite the burning anger at his presumption, despite her fury at his appalling arrogance, as she clipped on her seat belt, and though she'd never in a million years admit it, somewhere deep down inside Mia was relieved. A two-hour drive, even if it was in a luxury sports car, wasn't exactly at the top of her list. The day seemed to have caught up with her all of a sudden. Exhaustion saturated every pore, over-riding even the need for answers from Ethan, quelling slightly the utter force of his presence as they drove along the foreshore. But when they pulled up outside his ''property'', as her feet crunched on the smooth white stones beneath her feet the wealth and power that were Ethan Carvelle were rammed home yet again.

Why had she been naive enough to think they would be heading for some small luxury apartment in a nameless high-rise building? The residence they were entering now mocked that image a thousand times over. A massive white single-level home, chiselled so closely into the cliff edge she felt as if she could almost reach out and touch the pounding ocean that thundered below.

'I'll show you around…' Ethan started, but Mia shook her head.

'I don't need a guided tour, Ethan. I just want to know where I'm sleeping and tomorrow I'll go back to the hospital to have my blood pressure checked, then I'm out of here.' As he opened his mouth to argue she spoke over him. 'I know we need to talk, I know that's why I'm here after all, but I'm afraid it will have to wait till the morning.'

'What if it can't wait?' Ethan countered. 'What if I need some answers now?'

'Then you'll just have to exert some patience,' Mia responded firmly. 'My only priority at the moment is the baby, and, given I've spent the afternoon at a funeral and in hospital attached to a drip and monitors, I think it can be safely said that it's had quite enough drama for one day.' The fire seemed to die in her then, but she stood endearingly proud, in the massive lounge room, the wary defiance leaving her eyes as her shoulders slipped. She let out a long, weary sigh, fatigue literally overwhelming her, each word a feat in itself, weariness seeping into her bones, her eyes so heavy she just wanted to close them on this exhausting day, to start afresh tomorrow, to face Ethan for the last time with a clear mind and hopefully a less emotional heart. 'I just can't do this tonight, Ethan.'

'Fair enough.' His voice was the softest she'd heard it that day. 'But before you go to bed you should at least have something to eat.'

'I just want to sleep…'

'What have you eaten today?' he asked, watching as her forehead puckered into a tiny frown and, as much as it galled Mia to admit it, even to herself, Ethan had a point. The toast she'd listlessly made this morning had been thrown into the bin uneaten and she hadn't even thought about lunch as she'd driven into Cairns for the funeral, her mind too full of the events ahead to even contemplate eating.

'They gave me some sandwiches at the hospital.'

'Which were still sitting in their Cellophane when we left,' Ethan pointed out. 'If your priority really is the baby, then the very least you can do is go and sit down for half an hour and have something to eat and drink.'

She gave a small reluctant nod as Ethan slid open a massive glass door and walked out onto the balcony. After a moment's hesitation she followed him, chewing on her bottom lip as she stepped outside. The delicious view that greeted her tired eyes was so close to the first they had witnessed together it was almost painful just to look. A vast pool glittered before them, jutting out of the cliff top and in a clever architectural feat it seemed to merge in with the water, to kiss the ocean below. As exhausted as she was, if it had been anyone other than Ethan with her now she'd have been sorely tempted to peel off her clothes and float a while in the cool, clear water.

He led her to a table, pulled out a heavy wrought-iron chair and waited while she sat.

'Try and relax. I won't be long.'

Which was surely a joke!

How the hell was she supposed to relax even in this gorgeous setting while Ethan worked in the kitchen, when the man she both loved and loathed was, after all this time, a mere few feet away?

The darkness of the balcony gave her a chance to watch him unseen, to watch in breathless silence as he peeled off his black jacket, impatiently pulled off his tie, then rolled up the sleeves of his crisp white shirt, dark muscular forearms pulling open cupboards and working the massive stainless steel hob that would be any budding chef's dream. But from the occasional bang and cuss that broke the air, this luxury kitchen wasn't where Ethan spent much of his time and cooking clearly wasn't his forte.

Placing a plate of scrambled eggs and a massive glass of juice in front of her, he sat on the other side of the table, the silence deafening as he gazed broodily at the pool, before finally turning his headlights to her, her two minutes of down time clearly over as the interrogation recommenced.

'You're too thin,' he said for starters, as if his opinion mattered, as if he had every right to make such a personal observation. 'I suppose you're a vegetarian now!'

'Pardon?'

'Or a vegan perhaps,' Ethan sneered.

'You're amazing, Ethan.' Mia sighed. 'And, for the record, that wasn't a compliment. You really think you know me, don't you? You really think that because I'm an artist, because I've chosen to be a single mother, you can pigeon-hole me. Well, for your information, I'm neither a vegan nor a vegetarian, I don't attend peace rallies, I don't smoke dope...'

'I don't want your résumé, Mia,' Ethan snapped, clearly irritated. 'I'm merely pointing out that you're way too thin.'

'I know,' Mia admitted, pushing her eggs around the plate with a fork. 'But aside from what happened today, normally I eat very well. It's just that...'

'Just that what?' Ethan pushed as her voice trailed off.

'I guess I've been living on my nerves a bit the past few weeks.' Mia shrugged. 'Trying to hold my business together and visiting Richard every day.'

'How is business?' His shrewd eyes narrowed as he watched her closely.

'Good.' Mia looked up briefly, grateful for the safety of apparent small talk. 'I've been commissioned to do a series of pieces for a Japanese client and, as well as that, the gallery's really taken off.'

'You don't work from...*there* any more?' She heard the deviation in his voice, the slight hesitancy before the word. 'The studio, I mean.'

'It got too small.' She fiddled with her fork, took a mouthful of rather burnt egg before carrying on talking. 'That's why I moved out of Cairns. I couldn't afford a massive studio anywhere nearby so I bought a rather dilapidated house with stables and turned them into my work area. I've got heaps of space now.' She didn't add that the studio had held too many memories, how work had grown increasingly impossible as her mind had constantly wandered. How hard it had been to create magic with her hands as over and over the magic Ethan had created in that very space had taunted her mind. 'I kept the old place, though.'

'Why?'

'Sentimental reasons.'

'Which were?' In the darkness she couldn't be sure, but Mia was positive his cheeks darkened momentarily, and she felt a strange surge of triumph that Ethan Carvelle actually looked uncomfortable.

'It was just too hard to part with it in the end, given that my father had bought it for me.' It wasn't a lie, that had been the reason she hadn't sold it, the reason she'd practically begged the bank to let her hold onto it, dug in her heels and insisted she could afford both properties. But it was a lie by omission.

The time they had spent there, their first night together and the breathless nights and days that had followed, had been a huge factor in her desire to keep the place, the lingering memories devastating to keep but too precious to let go; though she certainly wasn't going to tell Ethan that, wasn't going to let his jumped-up ego inflate even a breath further.

'For ages it just stood there, had more than a few stones thrown through the window, but eventually the area picked up, a few cafés opened at first, followed by some up-market shops, and finally after all this time I now own a ''gallery'' to display my work in, which means the tourists assume I'm fabulously talented, when in fact I've just been fabulously lucky.'

'You are talented.' It was a statement, spoken in Ethan's usual clipped shorthand. No superfluous adjectives to dress it up, but the honesty behind his words, the mere fact he had said it, meant more to Mia than any review in the paper, any gushing appreciation of her work.

'You don't work there, though?' He registered her frown and gave a rather too casual shrug. 'I passed by it a few weeks ago and wandered in to have a look. I was greeted by a rather earnest young man with a beard that would have been more in place in biblical times—his sandals too. He said that he worked there and that the *artist* came in every now and then.'

Mia nodded, absolutely refusing to jump to his thinly veiled taunts. 'I employ a few art students from the uni; they share the roster between them.'

'Cheap labour.'

It was Mia's eyes narrowing now. 'We're not all just out to make money, Ethan. The reason I employ art students is because I'd rather have someone selling my work who actually understands the thought process behind it, and if they don't then at the very least they can, for the most part, accurately describe to clients the materials and methods used.'

'Sorry.' He grinned most annoyingly at her outburst, infuriating her even more.

'And for your information I pay them full wages. Furthermore, they have an area to display their own work, so, not only are they learning about the business side of things, they also have a chance to make some money and to showcase their talent.'

'Fantastic.'

Her fork paused midway to her mouth. She couldn't be positive, but she thought he was laughing at her, yet his eyes were earnest. He nodded at her to continue, and, after a moment's hesitation, Mia put down her fork and against her better judgment decided to give him the benefit of the doubt.

'It's hard for new artists to get a foot in the door.

This way, not only do they have a chance to be spotted, but the tourists can pick up some beautiful, original, local pieces for a relatively cheap price. It's a win, win situation.''

'Talent and a social conscience too.'

'You can have both,' Mia retorted, but she knew it was wasted, knew that in his infuriating way he had goaded her into this, that by pretending to be interested he had made a fool of her, had already won, that whatever she said now would just sound affected.

'I'm going to bed.' Pushing her plate away, she flung down her napkin and stood up.

'But you haven't finished your dinner.'

'Dinner!' Mia gave an incredulous snort. 'You call *that* dinner?' She knew she was being childish, knew that there were absolutely no points to be scored here, but she was past caring. 'You, Ethan Carvelle, can't even boil an egg.'

'They were scrambled.'

'Can't scramble an egg, then!'

'I have other talents!' Almost imperceptibly his lips twitched and Mia's eyes screwed closed, a furious blush scorching her cheeks. 'Still, if you look in the fridge I'm sure you'll find a jar of hollandaise sauce lurking there. A container too, perhaps. Maybe you could do a repair job on the eggs and take it down to your poor hungry students in the morning. Give them a teasing taste of the finer things in life to motivate them a touch more.'

'You're insufferable,' Mia snarled. 'Impossible and insufferable. I'm going to bed.'

'Second room on your left,' Ethan responded, completely unmoved, but as she made to go he caught her wrist, turning her around to face him and the teasing, superior look had left his eyes now, replaced instead with his harsh black stare, his fingers searing into her flesh as held her wrist in a vice-like grip. 'We'll talk tomorrow.'

'Fine.' She pulled at her arm but still he held her wrist.

'This *is* my brother's baby?'

She gave a frozen nod, then, as his free hand came up, as an unvoiced question darted in his eyes, she gave him reluctant permission to feel the child within her, closing her eyes as she felt his hot hand on her stomach, the baby swooping beneath his touch, and loneliness drowned her then. Missing at that moment all she could never have, a partner to be there for her, to guide her through this emotional time, to share in the milestones surely to come. And she felt a piercing sadness for the baby too, for all it would never now know.

The full white moon was shining down on her, the stars in the sky that now included Richard, and she missed him, not just for his friendship and love, but for her baby's sake, for the father it would never now see.

'Look after it, Mia.'

'I will.'

'I mean, look after yourself.'

She nodded her understanding, his hand moving reluctantly away, and she missed it as soon as it was gone, missed the strength and warmth of his touch, the tiny shared intimacy, even missed the vice of his grip on her wrist as he let it go.

His back was to the sky; in the darkness his expression was unreadable. 'Night, then,' she said, her voice slightly breathless, almost willing his hand back, almost willing him to touch her again, for this loneliness to end.

He didn't answer, and she didn't expect him to, slipping across the balcony and pulling open the door, reluctant to go but desperate to escape this emotional melting pot.

'Mia?' Something in his voice stilled her, something in his expression as she turned around made her want to weep, for never had she seen him so unsure, never had she seen Ethan anything other than confident and in control. 'Do you think he knew? Do you think he understood?'

'About the baby?' she checked, but Ethan shook his head.

'Do you think he knew he was loved?' Ethan's eyes searched hers. 'Deep down I mean. After I left Cairns we barely kept in touch, after he came back, after *I left*…' he faltered for a second before continuing '…everything changed between us and I never really understood why. I've been going over and over the visits to the hospice and I can't remember if I told him that I really did love him…' He gave a hollow laugh. 'I probably didn't.' The longest pause followed, his haughty face utterly still. 'I don't even know if I really believe in it.'

'He was loved,' Mia whispered. 'And I'm sure Richard knew it. He's at peace now, Ethan, you have to hold onto that. Although he was too young to die we both know that in the end it wasn't too soon—he's free of all that pain now and hopefully somewhere safe.'

And when she found her room, lay down on the cool sheets and stared at the relentless waves breaking on the shore, the moon drifting past, the world just carrying right on as before, even though Mia had thought it was over, that she'd expended her grief long, long before her dear friend had died, she knew then she had been mistaken. That the quiet tears that slid into her hair weren't for her baby, weren't for Ethan out there lonely and grieving on the balcony, weren't even for herself and for the love and friendship that had been taken too soon.

But for Richard.

For a man who was kind and gentle, a man who hadn't deserved to miss out on the precious years that should have been ahead.

'Are you sure about this?' Richard's incredulous voice seemed to whisper in the air around her as she recalled long-ago words that had sealed her fate; Richard pleased yet stunned at what she had agreed to, the commitment she'd been taking on just so that he might live. *'Are you sure you know what you're taking on, Mia?*

'Of course I'm sure.'

How naive she had been, how pathetically naive to think that the promises they had made as they'd stared into the fire that night wouldn't impact on her life for ever.

'No one must ever know the real reason, Mia!' Richard's usually gentle voice had been firm. 'We both have to promise that, no matter what happens, no matter the personal cost, we never reveal the reason for this pregnancy. It wouldn't be fair to the baby. If the truth came out it would make it sound so clinical, so calculating...'

'No one will ever know. I swear to you, Richard, that I'll never reveal that this baby was conceived by any other means than love.'

A different kind of love.

A different kind of love, which most people would never begin to understand.

Richard had been right to make her promise because it would be so easy now to tell Ethan the truth, so easy to exonerate herself, but at what cost to her child?

With tears sliding into her hair Mia stared into the darkness, feeling the baby swoop within, the innocent party in all this, the only one that really mattered.

Richard was gone now.

The secret was hers to keep.

CHAPTER FOUR

'The doctor's here.' Dropping one of his shirts on the bed, Ethan stared down at Mia. 'You can wear this.'

Startled eyes flashed open and for a second Mia truly thought she was dreaming, waking up to some delicious fantasy in which Ethan Carvelle still existed, the gorgeous white room she had barely taken in last night meriting more than a cursory glance. Dark jarrah floorboards were a delicious contrast to the white walls, void of even a single painting, the massive glass wall the only artwork needed, the endless expanse of ocean a stunning backdrop, but as her eyes dragged back to Ethan even the ocean paled beside his beauty.

He'd been swimming—a faint hint of chlorine hung in the air, clear eyes slightly bloodshot and sparkling from the water as black eyelashes clung together in short spikes. His hair was for once dishevelled, no doubt courtesy of the towel slung around his neck, the only thing he wore apart from another towel slung low on his waist, which begged a question in itself, the silky ebony line of hair on his flat, toned stomach leading suggestively downwards, teasing her mind as to what was underneath. And if she hadn't loathed him so much, if the history between them wasn't quite so vile, it would have been the easiest thing in the world to pull him into the bed beside her.

'What doctor?' Attempting to orientate herself to at least sound as if she were in some sort of control, Mia sat up, glancing at the bedside clock, appalled to see the hand edging towards eleven. 'I'm supposed to be at the hospital in five minutes.'

'Forget about the hospital,' Ethan responded. 'Garth Wilson is one of Cairns' leading obstetricians—well, according to my manager's wife, though I have to admit I have my reservations. He looks like one of your mob...'

'And what's that supposed to mean?' Mia retorted hotly as Ethan gave an annoying shrug.

'One of those peace-loving types. From my brief conversation he's into house calls and "*really* getting to know" his "*ladies*". Personally, I prefer my doctor in a suit with a mahogany desk between us.'

'That figures.' Mia sniffed.

'Anyway, I've checked all his credentials, which are pretty impressive, so I've asked him to take over your care.'

'Excuse me?' Mia would have stood, would have jumped right out of the bed and extended her five-feet-two frame for all it was worth, but given that she was wearing only a pair of panties she had to settle for sitting up with the sheet wrapped firmly around her and fixing Ethan with what she hoped was a withering stare. 'If I want a second opinion, then I'll arrange one myself. I certainly don't need you to do it on my behalf. Now, if you'll excuse me, I'd like to ring the hospital and see if I can reschedule my appointment.'

'Forget the hospital.' Ethan shook his head. 'Forget nameless faces looking after you. You need continuity of care…'

'Since when did you become such an expert on women's health?' Mia snapped, not waiting for a response before she carried on hotly. 'I don't want to hear another word about private obstetricians and home visits; there's absolutely no need for this.'

'Oh, I'd say there's every need.' In a surprising move he lowered himself from his rather menacing position standing over her and instead sat on the edge of the bed, his voice almost bordering on tender when he spoke. 'Mia, you're underweight, your blood pressure's through the roof and you collapsed yesterday due to dehydration.'

'I've explained all that,' Mia argued, but Ethan shook his head.

'You forgot to eat, Mia. Yes, it was Richard's funeral, yes, your mind was on other things, but you can't put everything down to yesterday. I don't know much about pregnant women but I'd hazard a guess that their weight is supposed to go up.'

'How do you know it hasn't?' Mia retorted. 'I've always been on the thin side.'

'No, you haven't.' He shook his head, one hand moving across the rumpled sheet, catching her calf through the cotton. Like a knee-jerk reaction, she went to pull it away, his touch more than she could bear, but Ethan held on tightly and she stared back at him, like a startled kitten. 'I've seen you, Mia, remember?'

And he did remember, every day, every night he remembered, and staring at her now, feeling the warmth of her leg through the sheet, it was so easy to drift back, to capture for a tiny second the moment it had all started.

The flash of the photographer, capturing the moment for ever as they had sat at the restaurant table. The weight of the world disappearing as they'd drifted off to a safer place that had been only for them. Feeding each other seafood as if they'd been together for ever, talking, laughing, feeling.

And later, when the only place to go had been further they had wandered away from the thrum of activity on the shore, away from the lights, along darker streets they'd walked, the buildings less attractive, the occasional drunk asleep in a doorway, until they'd come to a halt at some ugly metal roller doors.

'This is my studio.' Mia keyed in the combination. Ethan waited as the door slid up, ready to shake his head, to take her to some luxurious place where she surely belonged, but as he stepped inside, as she flicked on a light all Ethan knew was they were in the right place.

Every wall, every surface an extension of this delectable woman, every piece of dusty art that littered the tiny, cramped space as captivating and as inspiring as Mia.

'This is all your work.' He eyed the stacked canvases, the dusty benches filled with tiny sculptures.

'I sculpt.' She gave a tiny shrug. 'I paint as well.'

'These are beautiful.'

'But not perfect. I'm going to university this year, to study art…'

'Do you need to?'

She nodded. 'I need to learn more techniques. At the moment I'm just working on feelings; there are far more hits than misses…'

She was pulling at a ladder now, running it along the length of a back wall and climbing upwards, and the most sensible thing Ethan could do was turn and walk away, but instead he was following her up into the darkness, reaching the attic part of her studio, his eyes taking a moment to become accustomed to the darkness.

'Put on the light.'

'There are no lights up here,' Mia said softly, 'just the light from the bay. I don't normally sleep here, only if I'm caught up in a piece of work, sometimes I ring my father and tell him I'm staying over.'

He stared across at her, the sensible part of him struggling to make itself heard, but a low white bed was making itself known.

'I'm sorry.' She gave an apologetic shrug. 'It's way too messy; I should never have brought you here; I never bring anyone up here; I don't know what I was thinking…'

He could hear the sting of embarrassment in her voice, the heady, lust-induced euphoria of before ebbing away now. 'You must think I'm some sort of…'

She cleared her throat. 'Like I said—I've never brought anyone up here.'

'No one?'

She shook her head, blonde curls silver in the moonlight, her eyes glittering as she stared back at him.

'No one.' She swallowed hard. 'Before, in the restaurant, if I came on too strong…'

'You didn't,' Ethan said slowly.

'I just never expected to feel…' Again her voice trailed off, but the word hung in the air around them, the single word capturing again some of the magic that had imbued them.

She made him feel.

This stunning, mysterious, beautiful woman made him feel.

Ethan Carvelle was used to beautiful women, had made love to and rejected some of Australia's finest beauties; but not one of them held a candle to this bewitching jewel that forced his attention tonight, not one of them had even come close to lowering his guard in the way Mia had.

Reason and sensibility could go to hell.

He was twenty three years old, for God's sake; she was over the age of consent.

This wasn't wrong.

'You're beautiful.' He'd never said it to a woman before, normally it was Ethan on the receiving end of compliments, but she made honesty so easy. 'Tell me, Mia, what do you want?'

She blinked back at him, the moonlight catching her

dangling earrings, shimmering against her long neck as she swallowed hard.

'I want you to make love to me.' He could see her eyes widening, heard a tiny nervous giggle as if she couldn't believe what she had just said.

'Go on.' His voice was thick and low, his breath so shallow he had to remind himself to slow it down.

'I want you to show me how.'

'You've never made love before?'

She shook her head. He could see her cheek darkening, feel her embarrassment and though he ached to soothe it, wanted only to lay her on the massive white bed and grant her wish with no questions asked, still a piece of him held back.

'What about Richard?'

'We're friends, Ethan, that's all.'

And he believed her.

'Richard and I are just good friends, nothing more than that…' She gave a tiny shrug, the movement in her shoulders causing her breasts to lift invitingly, causing the buds of her nipples to graze against her dress, and he bit back a physical need to cross the room, to hush that full mouth with a heavy kiss, but he had asked the question, the least he could do was listen to her answer. *'I don't expect anything from you, Ethan. In a couple of months I go to uni; once you've found Richard you'll be back in Sydney. I know we're worlds apart…'*

She never finished, he couldn't let her, crossing the space in an instant, his lips crushing down on hers, drowning out her last gasps of reason, his expert

*tongue searching the hollows of her throat, holding
her needy body against his. Her lips sweeter, more
precious than anything he had ever tasted in his life,
kissing her back with a depth and passion he hadn't
known he was capable of. Pulling the pins from her
hair till the blonde locks cascaded down, feeling the
cool curtain in one hand as he wrestled with the zipper on her dress, sliding it down over her shoulders,
his arousal so furious it hurt. Seeing her standing
before him, no bra, the white pearls of her tiny
breasts, soft and ripe and plump against her toned
body, with just a tiny pair of panties. He pulled the
silken garment aside and, seeing the delicate blonde
of her bush, he thought he would explode in anticipation.*

*That she was here, that he could have her, that this
divine, delectable creature wanted him as much as he
did her, was almost more than he could fathom. But
he dragged on every last reserve of control, pulling
back slightly, taking her soft, tiny breasts in his hot
hand as the other slipped her panties down, running
a hand over the hollows of her stomach, fingers
lightly brushing the soft blonde hair, his tongue on
her flat, quivering stomach enough force alone to
guide her softly onto the bed. He knelt over her, taking his time, focusing for a decadent moment on each
breast, whispering soft endearments into ears more
beautifully shaped than any shell on the beach. His
experienced fingers found her private jewel, worked
it slowly, rhythmically, the palm of his hand grazing
her swollen mound, feeling her quiver under his*

touch, working the moist warmth till the nervous gasp that had first emanated from her lips turned into low moans of desire, snaking his fingers gently inside as her gasps grew louder, bringing her ever closer to the edge with masterful fingers. If it had been anyone else, he would have taken her then, would have given into his own furious desire and plunged his length inside, but he wanted more for her, wanted so much more, so instead of his own needs he concentrated on hers.

Burying his head in that sweet glistening pool, he was rewarded tenfold, the ecstatic cries the feel of her thighs quivering against his cheeks more of an aphrodisiac than he could have imagined. Ethan knew he couldn't hold back a second longer, scared of hurting her, that his furious, rampant arousal might pain her virgin flesh, but she was so wonderfully wet and warm and receiving as he thrust inside; crying out his name as he called out hers, wrapping lithe legs around him as he plunged ever deeper. He exploded at the first thrust, feeling her spasm around him, her whole body rigid as he delved further inside her, and he never wanted it to end, never wanted to go back to where he had been, wanted this shuddering ecstasy, this heady moment to go on for ever, to never lose the memory, the feeling of holding Mia in his arms.

Normally he hated talking, normally he rolled over, stared into the night and just wished the face on the pillow would be quiet, wished that he didn't resent the woman who lay beside him, wished he could just get the hell out of there and go.

But not tonight.

Tonight he rolled onto his other side, faced the woman who lay beside him, with not a tinge of shame or regret to sully what had taken place.

'Ethan. Thank you.'

A lazy smile inched over his face. 'For what?'

'For making love to me, for…'

'I haven't finished yet.' He could feel the stirrings starting already, the feel of her, the sound of her, the scent of her enough, more than enough, to arouse him all over again, and right there and then Ethan knew she had nothing to do with whatever her father was up to, knew beyond a shadow of a doubt that she wasn't involved in Richard's disappearance. Most pointedly of all as he stared back at that innocent, beautiful face he could think of a million worse things than being tied to her for ever. 'In fact we've barely started.'

He meant it.

At that moment he would have promised her anything, given her the world if only she would let him.

If only Richard hadn't come back…

'Ethan.' Mia's pale whisper pulled Ethan sharply back to reality.

'You can't compare my body now to how it was then…'

Mia didn't want to remember, didn't want to cloud the issue with the ghosts of their past, didn't want what they had once shared in any way to impinge on the decisions she made today, and it wasn't fair of Ethan to bring the past up now, not when there was a doctor waiting outside, not when there was absolutely no chance of seeing the conversation through to its entirety. 'I was eighteen, Ethan.'

She could feel the heat of his hand searing through the sheet, feel the caress of his fingers on the back of her calf, the nub of his thumb pressing into her flesh, and she knew he felt it too, knew he was remembering all that had taken place between them. The primitive, animal arousal in the air was so thick she could almost taste it, but as her words hit their mark Ethan moved his hand away, dropping contact as if he were touching hot coals, his eyes opening and fixing her with a warning glare.

'I wasn't.' His voice was full of scorn. 'I wasn't,' he repeated as if saying it again might somehow alter the truth. 'I was referring to the fact that I've seen you arriving and leaving at the hospice these past few weeks, nothing else. Nothing else!' he said again, only more loudly this time. His hand that had just touched her clenched so tightly the knuckles were white, eyes furious with his blatant denial, and Mia lay reeling, appalled that even the memory of that night could trigger such a fierce response in him.

'You owe it to the baby to see this doctor,' he said in a more reasonable voice. 'You need proper care and clearly whatever you've been getting hasn't been sufficient.'

She gave a tiny, reluctant nod. 'Okay, I'll see him,

but I'm warning you, Ethan, this is my pregnancy and my baby. I won't have you interfering. I mean it,' she added firmly, but Ethan just stood up.

'Let's see what the doctor says, shall we?'

'Lose the *we*, Ethan.' She watched his hand pause on the handle, saw the dart of frustration in his eyes as he turned around. '*I'll* see the doctor and then *I'll* make up my own mind.'

He gave a small nod, made to go, then changed his mind, determined to have the last word. 'At the very least keep an open mind, Mia. Listen to what he has to say before you form an opinion.'

'That's a bit rich coming from you, Ethan.' The door was almost closed behind him, but she shot out her response, equally determined to say her piece.

Yet despite her secret intention to remain suitably unimpressed with the undoubtedly expensive private obstetrician Ethan had infuriatingly chosen for her, Mia saw in an instant why Garth Wilson was so successful with his *'ladies'*. In contrast to her rather brief visits with any given doctor at the local hospital, going over and over her antenatal history to an unfamiliar face, Garth instantly put her at ease, taking his time to listen to her before finally examining her, and his care didn't end there. He sat on the edge of the bed and carefully went through her birthing options, happily open to her suggestions for as natural a birth as possible.

'I'd have liked to have had the baby at home, of course…' Mia swallowed '…but…'

'Given your raised blood pressure it's probably not

the safest way to go.' Garth smiled warmly. 'The birthing centre is an excellent option; the midwives are very in tune…' His eyes frowned in concern. 'Is there something else, Mia? Something you want to tell me?'

'There is, but…' Her voice trailed off, hesitancy in every word that followed, unsure whether to go on, yet knowing she had to. 'It mustn't go any further; I mean, if I tell you, Ethan mustn't—'

Garth put up a very well-manicured hand, which seemed out of place given his casual attire. 'It stays here.' He tapped his rather scruffy head. 'So what's troubling you, Mia?'

'Nothing.' She shook her head but it changed midway. 'Everything,' she admitted, biting back a batch of tears. 'Even though the idea of a home birth appeals, I'd always planned to have the baby at hospital because we were going to use the cord blood…'

'Use the cord blood?' Garth asked perceptively. 'As opposed to donating it?'

Mia gave a tiny, trembling nod. 'The baby's father had cancer.'

'Ethan isn't the father?' She watched his eyebrow furrow, but Garth quickly righted himself. 'Hey, sorry, he just came across as so concerned…'

'This is his brother's baby, *that's* why Ethan is so concerned. Richard died last week; we cremated him yesterday.'

'Mia, I'm sorry.' Garth looked truly appalled at her revelation, his eyes blinking in rapid confusion at her apparent lack of reaction. 'You must still be in shock…'

'It was expected,' Mia responded.

'But even so.' Garth eyed her in concern. 'To lose your partner at this precious time…'

'Please!' A trembling hand halted him as Mia struggled to gain control. Garth's misdirected sympathy was the last thing she needed right now. No one on God's earth understood her relationship with Richard and that was how they'd wanted it, that was how they had promised each other it would be whatever the personal cost. All she wanted from Garth was his medical skills, nothing else.

Nothing else.

'I still want the blood to be used, though; I'd like it to be donated to the cord bank. Richard and I spoke about it; we both decided…' Her voice trailed off, cold facts all she was prepared to reveal. 'Will you be able to arrange that for me, Garth?'

'Of course.' Garth nodded, patting her arm, still clearly confused at her apparent cool demeanor. 'I can take care of all that for you. There will just be a mountain of paperwork for you to sign and a few blood tests nearer the end of your pregnancy and again a few months after…'

'And Ethan won't know?'

'Not if you don't want him to.' The frown remained on his brow. 'Is there anything else you want to tell me, Mia? Anything at all?'

'Nothing.' Her eyes glittered with unshed tears, the weight of her secret so heavy on her tired shoulders, but she swallowed them down, her chin jutting defiantly as she stared directly back at him, the secret inside not just hers to reveal. 'Nothing at all.'

It was a full hour before Garth left the bedroom with a timely reminder undoubtedly ringing in his ears that Ethan might be footing the bill, but he had no right to her personal information.

'Well?' As she slipped out of bed and the huge oversized shirt he had loaned her and padded to the *en suite* Ethan caught her unawares, marching in the bedroom unannounced as Mia gave a furious yelp and dived into the *en suite* to grab a towel, returning a second or two later, cheeks flaming but thankfully almost decent. From Ethan's impatient stance he clearly thought he was entitled to some answers.

He was dressed in a suit, his hair neatly combed now, a tie hanging around his neck waiting to be knotted, shoes on his feet with the laces still undone, and he looked every bit as sexy as the semi-naked man she had opened her eyes to an hour ago. 'What did he say?'

'Who?'

She saw his eyes narrow, heard his sharp intake of breath. 'Don't be facetious, Mia. I've got a meeting in half an hour and I want to know what's going on before I leave. We'll talk properly when I get back; so quickly, please: what did the doctor say?'

'I thought patient confidentiality extended beyond the signature on the cheque.'

The air hissed out of his lungs, his face contorting

as he attempted to stay calm, knowing if he inflamed her further then he'd find out nothing. 'Mia—' his voice was very soft, very low, but she could feel the tension behind every last word '—could you please tell me what the doctor said?'

'That my blood pressure's still up.'

'And?'

'That I need to slow down.'

'And?'

'That apart from that everything's fine.'

'Mia, he was in here for the best part of an hour; surely he said more than that.'

'Look, Ethan.' Exasperated, she ran a hand through her chaotic hair, embarrassed by his scrutiny, desperate to put some space between them, for him to go to his blessed meeting and leave her alone with her jumbled thoughts, to try and make sense of the chaotic situation she had found herself in. Where one move, one thoughtless slip, and the whole pack of lies she and Richard had so carefully built would come tumbling down. 'It's been seven years since I've seen you. You can't expect me to just open up to you.'

'Why not?' He truly sounded as if he didn't know and Mia shook her head in disbelief, stunned at the arrogance of him.

'After the way you treated me, you expect to swan in and demand information, demand personal details as if it were your God-given right. You have the gall to expect me just to bare all and ''quickly please'', just because you've got a business meeting.'

'After the way I treated you?' Ignoring her last few

words, he crossed the room, blocking the entrance to the *en suite*, his huge shoulders blocking the door-frame. 'You're the one with gall, Mia! The absolute audacity to stand there and twist things, to make it sound as if you were the wronged party all those years ago! So tell me, Mia, just what is it I'm supposed to have done? Where exactly do you feel you were treated badly?' His voice was rising with each and every word, the confrontation she'd been simulta-neously needing and dreading clearly a breath away, and Mia wasn't sure she was ready, wanted at least to be dressed before the ugly truth was exposed.

'You slept with me, Ethan. Those weeks we shared meant everything to me. You said that you loved me, adored me, wanted to be with me, and all the time you were using me. All the time you were planning to sack my father, using me to find out where Richard was, and I fell for it.'

'I was the one who fell,' Ethan roared. 'I was the idiot who fell for every lie you fed me.'

'I never lied,' Mia begged, but Ethan was shaking his head, black eyes glittering with seven years of unvented fury. 'You were the liar. Richard came back and you left. Not only that but you sacked my father two days later. You squeezed your pound of flesh from me and left me with nothing.'

'Nothing!' His voice was like the crack of the whip. 'Nothing?'

'I'd like a shower, please, Ethan.' Her voice was supremely calm. 'And if you won't let me have one, then I'll damn well get dressed and take a taxi back to my own home this very minute.'

Amazingly he moved, just enough to let her past, but his angry eyes were still on her, his body still in the doorway, and suddenly Mia had had enough.

'I'm going to have a shower now, Ethan.'

'You're damn well not,' Ethan barked. 'If you think you can toss a little gem like that at me and then walk off, then you've got another think coming. I left you with a damn sight more than you left me. I treated you so much better than you deserved, Mia Stewart. If it wasn't for me you'd be on the streets now, not in some fancy gallery calling yourself an artist. And the pay-out the Carvelles gave your father was so, so much more than he deserved!'

Mia swung around, her livid eyes meeting his, her mouth set in a taut pale line, her face menacingly close as she hissed the words out. 'Leave my father out of this, Ethan, or I swear I'll...'

'What? Come on, Mia, what can you possibly say that might change things when we both know that I've treated you a damn sight better than *you* deserve? I could have thrown you and your family to the lions, but instead I persuaded my father against calling the police, practically begged him to pay out your father rather than sack him!'

'Sack him!' It was Mia's voice rising now, Mia staring with incredulous disbelief at this hateful man. 'For what? Because his daughter was screwing the boss?' Even though they came from her own lips the coarseness of her words shocked Mia, but this was what he'd forced her into, this was the result of Ethan reducing what had been beautiful to nothing more than a sordid sexual encounter.

'Screwing the Carvelle family, more like!' Ethan's face was as white as the tiles that lined the bathroom, his eyes dark, angry pools that glittered menacingly. 'Screwing, not just one, but two of the brothers…'

'What?'

'You were sleeping with us both.' She shook her head, opened her mouth to speak, but Ethan got there first. 'Don't play the innocent, Mia. Yes, I went back to my parents' home when I heard Richard was back, but I wasn't intending to leave you, I was going to tell them…' His fists bunched by his sides, his temples pounded with the roar of his own pulse as he remembered striding up the drive. Ready to face whatever Richard had been up to head-on, to soothe troubled waters with good news.

He had loved her.

'You were going to tell them what?' Mia dragged him back to the present and he stared at her coolly, shaking his head, unable to believe he had really been so naive.

'Hedging your bets, were you?' He gave a low, mirthless laugh as her face twisted in confusion. 'You couldn't lure Richard back into bed so figured you'd settle for his older brother?'

'I've no idea what you're talking about.'

'I heard it from his own mouth, Mia! I heard Richard telling my parents that he was mixed up with you, that that was why he'd run away, that was why he'd left town as if the devil himself was chasing him. He was terrified you were pregnant, terrified you'd trapped him…'

'You're disgusting.'

'No, you're disgusting,' Ethan roared. 'You used me, slept with me with the sole intention of getting pregnant because you knew that your father was about to go to prison. Both you and your father were screwing us for every last cent. Your father was a con artist, Mia; you know it as well as I do. Your father was spending the firm's money more quickly than he could cover it and we trusted him, Mia, trusted him enough not to look over his shoulder, but at what price? He cost the Carvelles hundreds of thousands of dollars…'

'He saved the precious Carvelles! He saved you all from finding out a truth you didn't want to hear.' Her words were out before her thought process had even finished, the lid of Pandora's box springing open and even if she could close it, even if she could take it back, Mia wasn't sure she wanted to. To hear her father's name sullied, to hear Ethan Carvelle besmirching the wonderful, kind man her father had been was almost more than Mia could take. Fury, anger, hurt lacing each and every word, her face twisting in rage as she let Ethan have it, she felt a curious surge of triumph as her words hit their target, rocking the Carvelle pedestal for just a tiny moment. 'He saved you from finding out the truth!'

'Go on.' His voice was even, his face almost impassive, only the pulse pounding in his cheek told her that Ethan was anything other than calm. 'Don't start something you can't finish, Mia.'

'Oh, I can finish it, Ethan.' Pulling the towel tighter around her breasts, she stared at him defiantly. 'I can finish it right here and now, so long as you're sure you want to hear it.' A tiny nod was the only response she got, and the voice that had been laced with venom only seconds earlier was curiously flat now, her lips pale as she ran a dry tongue over them. 'My father wasn't spending the firm's money, as your family were so quick to accuse.'

'I've still got the financial records,' Ethan retorted. 'Your father was siphoning money. He was good; I have to hand it to him. He covered his tracks remarkably well, but in the end I spotted it.' He watched as she shook her head, a surprising glint of pity in his eyes as still she refused to accept the facts.

'You've got it all wrong,' she insisted.

'If you want I can show the records to you; your father—'

'I don't need to see the records…' Mia jumped in and she watched his mouth move, watched it open and snap closed, took a deep breath before she carried on. 'My father wasn't stealing from the company—'

'Oh, for heaven's sake, Mia,' Ethan broke in, 'this is getting us nowhere. You know the truth, I know the truth, so why keep up the pretence? Why not just admit that you were using me? Why not just admit that your father—'

'It was Richard.'

'Richard?' His face twisted in rage as she stared

back at him, appalled at what she'd said, but relieved as well. 'Is that how low you're prepared to stoop, Mia? Blame a dead man—'

'Richard's not the only dead man,' Mia interrupted. 'My father went to his grave knowing you all believed he'd stolen from you. My father carried the secret for five long years and finally it killed him. So don't you dare stand there and judge him; don't you dare stand there and call him a con artist. Unlike your family, my father actually cared. He knew that if the great Hugh Carvelle found out his son was in financial difficulty the hell he'd put Richard through. The only crime my father committed was covering Richard's tracks.'

'Which is a crime in itself,' Ethan quipped, but his voice had lost all its certainty, his breathing short and ragged as he surveyed the past with the benefit of hindsight. 'Richard had money problems?'

Mia gave a hesitant nod, wondering just how much to reveal. 'Richard had huge money problems at that time, Ethan. Huge,' she added, biting her lip as she recalled the awful time, the anguish in her friend's eyes when he had broken down and confessed the sordid ugly truth, the same raw anguish that was in Ethan's eyes now, and she couldn't do it—couldn't pull back the skin on another layer of pain, couldn't bring herself to tell Ethan just how bad it had really been, tell him about the so-called friends who had been bribing Richard, the sordid videos that probably didn't exist, but whose mere hint at their existence had been enough to force Richard into serious debt.

But it wasn't only Ethan's feelings she was saving by diluting the truth; revealing all about Richard's plight could only bring Ethan one step closer to her own truth.

'Richard was in a mess when he came back. It was only after my father had been sacked, after you'd left that, I found out what had been going on.'

'Why, though?' Ethan asked, visibly perplexed. 'Why didn't your father tell the truth when we confronted him? Why didn't he tell us what had been happening instead of carrying the can for Richard?'

'Because, as you so delicately pointed out, covering Richard's tracks was a crime in itself. He had hoped, of course, that when the truth came out Hugh would understand his reasons.'

'Only the truth never came out?'

She stared back at him for an age before answering, her lips so taut they barely moved when finally she spoke.

'Contrary to the firing squad he was expecting to face when the debts were uncovered, my father received a handsome pay-out accompanied naturally with a lot of legal jargon which he didn't understand.' Choking back humiliation, she forced herself to look at him. 'But *I* did, Ethan. Especially the clause about relationships real or implied. I believe that was aimed at me, wasn't it, Ethan?'

'It was a damned good deal,' Ethan responded, but the assuredness had gone from his voice now. 'You might not believe this, Mia, but as much as I loathed what you'd done, I still fought for you. We could have left you with nothing, dragged in the police...'

'Sometimes I wish you had,' Mia said softly. 'As much as I loved Richard, it took a long time for me to forgive him for what he put my father through.' She closed her eyes for a painful second. 'But the truth would have hurt us all.' She gave a hollow laugh. 'What happened to the man who held me, Ethan? What happened to the man who said that he believed in me and that come what may we'd face it together?'

'He grew up,' Ethan said darkly. 'Right around the time he came home and found out that the beautiful woman he thought he knew, the woman he'd held in his arms and made love to, the woman he'd have given anything, *anything* to be with had been using the same charms, playing the very same game, with his brother.

'I wouldn't have given a damn about your father's debts, Mia. I'd have been there with you through it all, whatever the personal cost...'

'Then why did you leave?' Mia begged. 'You're standing there telling me you could have dealt with it, yet you walked away, Ethan. Why?'

'Because some things are just too abhorrent to forgive...' He saw the frown collect on her brow and it infuriated him. 'When Richard came back I went to my parents' house, Mia. I was ready to tell them I loved you, ready to take whatever they dished out about your father and stand by you...' He dragged in a breath through taut, pale lips. 'I overheard Richard telling my parents that there was a very good chance you were pregnant by him.'

'By Richard? How on earth could I possibly have been pregnant by Richard?'

The incredulity in her voice only angered him further.

'Do you want a biology lesson, Mia? God, I know you were only eighteen, but from the memory I have of our time together you certainly knew the difference between a man and a woman.'

'I've *never* slept with Richard!' Her words were barely out before her hand shot to her throat. She gasped at the heavy air as if she were trying to reel them back, to retract the terrible truth, but Ethan pounced like a hungry lion on his prey, tearing her to shreds with his sharp tongue, cross-examining her with all the stealth of the prosecutor of the accused.

'You've never slept with Richard!' His statement gave her no room for manoeuvre as he walked the short distance towards her, his breath scorching her cheeks as he drew in close. 'Forgive me for sounding cynical, Mia, but I need some clarification here. Seven years ago, Richard was scared that you'd trapped him, running as if the devil was chasing him because he thought you were pregnant with his child. Seven years on you're telling me that, not only are you pregnant by him, not only did you have his loving consent, but lo and behold now you're telling me that you've never slept with him. So come on...' His hand gripped her upper arm, and even though there was no violence in his fingertips, even though his touch was feather-light, she could feel the mental rattling, the stern shake for an answer. 'Enlighten me. What the hell happened between you two? Is this or is this not Richard's child?'

She could feel her pulse pounding in her temples, almost hear the thud of her eyelashes batting together as she struggled with the web that tightened around her; she knew that her response, those next few words, was one she would have to live with for the rest of her life.

'It is.' A dry tongue ran over even dryer lips, his black eyes boring into her skin, registering every flicker of her reaction.

'You know there are tests? Once this baby's born it will only be a matter of time…'

'I don't need tests…' Furious eyes met his, furious, defiant eyes, like a wary kitten backed into the corner, lashing out at a piece of string, fighting everything that came in its path. 'I don't need tests to confirm what I know in here.' Her hand thumped her heart, pride laced in every word. 'All I can tell you is that, whatever Richard said that night, whatever you over-heard, I didn't sleep with him all those years ago, Ethan. All I can tell you is that you *were* my first lover; you were my—'

'Fool!' He hurled the word at her like a missile, humiliation, torture, regret the wind that carried it, seven years of buried pain more deadly than any nuclear warhead. 'I'm the fool for standing here listening to your pathetic arguments. I was *your* fool, Mia. I believed you that night when you said I was the first and tumbled into bed with you after you'd slept with my brother!' His voice rose to a frenzied peak, agony etched on every feature. 'My God, Mia, how low did you expect me to stoop? How low does a man have to go for you to get your kicks? Richard is my brother, you came from his bed to mine…'

'No!' With supreme dignity she shook her head and stared at him as if she were looking into his very soul, before she said it again. 'No, Ethan, you're wrong. Whatever he said, whatever you choose to believe, you have to know this. That first night…' The words lingered in the air, crackled between them for a tangible moment, *that night* too precious to relegate to a throwaway comment, *that first night* branded on their souls, etched in their memories, deserving so much more than a cursory mention. She faltered a moment, struggled to regain her composure as memories danced in the static air between them. 'When we met, when we…' a tiny swallow, a strangled, choking gesture as she struggled to get past it, to move the conversation past this dangerous, treacherous road '…Richard and I were friends at that time. Nothing more, nothing less.

'I couldn't have been pregnant by Richard, because I'd never slept with him.'

And something in her stance, something in her eyes told him she was speaking the truth. 'Then why would he…?' His voice trailed off. He was for once completely lost for words, his eyes beseeching her to help him, to shed some light, but Mia just stood there. 'I don't understand, Mia.'

'Your parents obviously knew that he was in trouble,' she said softly, 'knew something was troubling him, and no doubt they wanted an answer?'

He gave a small nod.

'Maybe that was all he could come up with, maybe with his back against the wall it was the only excuse he could come up with to explain…'

'He mentioned your father's name…' Ethan's eyes narrowed as he recalled the conversation, horrible clarity invading, the benefit of hindsight agony now, remembering the fear in Richard's voice. 'He was trying to tell them the mess he was in, trying to explain…'

'But he couldn't,' Mia finished for him. 'Couldn't bring himself to see it through, to reveal to your father what was really troubling him, so instead he panicked and said the first thing that came into his head, maybe said something your father would have preferred to hear—that he thought he'd got some girl pregnant.

'Unfortunately for us, he chose to use me,' Mia finished simply.

'I'd have helped him, Mia.' He made a small confused sound, halfway between a sob and a sigh, hands raking his hair over and over. 'Why didn't he come to me if he needed money?'

She stared back at him, a breath away from telling him everything, but holding it deep inside. Revealing Richard's truth would only expose her own. Her hands fluttered to her stomach in a protective gesture as she willed the conversation over, for this interrogation to end.

'Some things are best left, Ethan. Some—'

'Mia, please,' Ethan started, but she shook her head.

'I can't do this, Ethan. You want to know what the doctor said, then here it is: I need rest, I need to stay calm, need to keep my blood pressure down, and dredging over the past isn't going to help anyone.'

'It might.'

'And it might not!' Mia responded. 'Ethan, I need some space, some time to think. Go to your meeting, do whatever it is you have to do. Right now, I'm going to have my shower.'

But her words didn't move him, not an inch.

Fine, Mia decided, if Ethan Carvelle didn't have the decency to leave then he could damn well stay. The towel still safely around her, she turned on the shower, praying he'd take his cue and leave, but Ethan clearly had other ideas.

'I'm not leaving till I have some answers, Mia.' His voice was loud over the water, his stance supremely confident, but so was Mia. Dropping the towel, she shot him a defiant look. Utterly refusing to blush, she pulled the glass door open and stepped into the shower, satisfied that his expensive suit and his Italian leather shoes would keep him at bay. She registered a furious bellow of rage, but she refused to be intimidated, a strange exhilaration filling her.

So Ethan wanted to be involved with her pregnancy—well, see how he felt at the sight of her seven months pregnant! Lathering her hair, she closed her eyes, utterly refusing to be rushed, and when his rantings got louder it was easier to sing, easier to turn her back on the fire she had just ignited, than face the explosive truth. But Ethan had other ideas. Aghast, she swung around as six feet four of fully dressed indignation stepped in the shower beside her, holding her shoulders and demanding she face him.

'You can't come in here,' Mia yelped.

'I'm already in,' he snarled, one hand clutching her shoulder the other forcing her chin up to make her look at him. 'You'll damn well look at me and tell me what you know.'

'I can't.'

'You will,' he roared.

'I can't see, Ethan.' Somewhere between fury and outrage, the ire died in his eyes, the questions that had been so important only seconds before coiling into the air along with the steam as she let out a giggle that was entirely out of place given the circumstances. Even Ethan managed a reluctant laugh as she accepted the handkerchief he pulled from his suit and wiped the rivers of soapy lather out of her eyes. The bizarreness of their situation finally caught up. Heavily dressed and heavily pregnant, they stood in the shower and when finally Mia's world came back into focus it was softer and gentler but infinitely more dangerous.

'Richard lied?' he checked and she nodded, watched the regret that tinged his solemn face as he digested her response.

'I let you go…'

'You didn't let me go,' she reminded him painfully.

'You pushed me away, Ethan. You refused to return my calls or respond to my letters, left me hanging in limbo for ages, wondering what on earth I'd done wrong, what I possibly could have said that deserved such appalling treatment. It should have been so beautiful, Ethan. We could have been there for each other, facing those terrible times together, dealt with the mess Richard had created as a team, but instead you left me to deal with it alone…'

'I'm sorry.'

He meant it. And maybe two little words shouldn't have sufficed, maybe two little words shouldn't have been able to wipe out seven years of torture, but such was the regret, the honesty behind the words, she knew he meant it.

The water beat relentlessly on. And when Ethan's eyes finally opened, slowly working the length of her body, the row, the horrors of the past were pushed aside. Now as his eyes drifted over her he decided whoever said pregnancy wasn't sexy clearly hadn't been there, because never had a body looked more ripe or overtly feminine. The tiny budding breasts he had touched all that time ago were gone now, replaced instead with the heavy ripeness of pale flesh, the pink of her areola circling a gloriously jutting nipple, rivers of water cascading between her cleavage leading his gaze to the naked swell of her abdomen. His gaze was almost reverend as he saw the taut skin, his fingers tentative as they moved to touch it, only this time he didn't need to ask permission, this time it was Mia's hand guiding his, watching his reaction as his hand met the soft swell, taking in the emotion on his face as he traced the outline of the tiny life within.

'You've got a meeting,' Mia reminded him softly.

'*Had* a meeting,' Ethan corrected. 'I can hardly go in like this…'

'I'm sure there's plenty more where this came from.' Her fingers toyed with the lapels of his jacket, her eyes closing in ecstasy as his face moved down to hers. The haven of the dreams that had sustained her didn't hold a candle to the feel of his heavy lips finally on hers. The water saturating each potent kiss couldn't dilute the ecstasy, his hand on the small of her back, pulling her in towards him, her swollen breasts pressed against his chest, her full stomach pressing in, the length of his fierce erection against her thigh intoxicating as she pressed harder against him.

Sweet, sweet memories cascaded in, mingling with new ones that were created here and now, an affirmation that what had taken place before *had* been real, that the overwhelming beauty she had witnessed once hadn't merely been seen through the rose-colored glasses of youth, but had been as real and as divine as the dreams that had captured them. The exquisite taste of his mouth on hers, no contempt in familiarity as she explored the velvet of his lips, the sharp taste of his tongue, felt again the rivers of lust rippling through her body, the arousal Ethan Carvelle so easily instigated. The fierce desire that had been waiting impatiently in the wings for so long now ran unhindered onto stage, dancing freely, moving instinctively. She remembered, *remembered* the intensity of his touch, how one brush of his skin on hers could spin her into a balmy orbit, the thrum of pulses like the bass in the orchestra, always there, holding the rhythm, pushing it forward, deepening the intensity as his needy mouth devoured hers as his.

It was Ethan who broke the contact.

Ethan who pushed her away, who shook his head in almost repulsion, as if waking from some terrible dream, as if scarcely able to comprehend what had taken place. She felt the shudder of his muscles, the controversy in every movement as he pushed with his hands but pleaded with his eyes, every fibre that bound them, every breath saturated with the passion that had gripped them, but the sobering slap of reality too strong to ignore.

'You…' The water lashed his face, rivers running down that strong jaw, like tears of regret; the push of his palms, the grip of his fingers, confusion, pain in every tortured gasp. 'You make me crazy.' She could feel every breath in his arms, exasperation, regret tingeing every motion, the steel of his erection against her thighs, the soft marshmallow of her flesh melting against him, an expensive suit no barrier against his deadly sword. 'You make it so easy to be wrong.' She could see the white of his teeth as he clenched them together, feel the agony behind every word. 'You make it too damn easy to throw it all away…

'Throw what away?' Her question was genuine. Whether it was love or lust, something propelled them, something drove them to this edge over and over, yet here he was—pulling back, pushing her over into the abyss of life without him, and from the desolation in his eyes, from the pounding thud of her heart, it didn't matter who delivered the fatal wound because agony gripped them both.

'Everything.' He shook his head fiercely. 'Morals, duty, loyalty. You, Mia, shame me over and over.'

'How?'

'By making me want you!'

And she knew, knew from the way his hands dropped her, knew from the step back he took that it was all over. But still she couldn't admit defeat.

'I want you too, Ethan.' Trembling hands reached for him, honesty a whisper away, denial useless as she faced the full force of the arousal that gripped them, the arousal that saturated them, that was instigated by their mere presence together. 'I have for seven years. For seven years I've wanted you. Seven years,' she rasped. 'And I know you want me too. Surely we can find a way to make it work; surely we can get past all this?' He could feel the swell of the baby between them, between them in so many more ways than merely physical. His brother's baby bringing them together on the one hand, yet tearing them apart with the other.

His brother's baby.

Images he didn't want to think about, couldn't bring himself to witness, were homing in: that he had practically forced her into Richard's arms by his cruel rejection, by his utter failure to ask her side of events.

A painful lesson he had well and truly learnt, but it was too late now, for remorse or for what might have been. His brother's baby was growing inside the woman he loved, his brother had held her, made love to her, adored her. And, whatever way he looked at it, Richard had been cremated less than twenty-four hours.

Black pools of bile churned inside him as the ramifications hit home, the almost incestuous edge a coupling would bring, too close for moral comfort.

'It's too late for us, Mia.'

'Maybe not,' she whispered. 'Ethan—'

'It's too late,' he broke in. 'This is Richard's baby and I know...' he closed his eyes in regret before continuing '...that I'll never get past that fact.'

'Is it the fact it's Richard's baby or that Richard and I...?' Her voice trailed off. She knew she was tipping the conversation into dangerous territory and held back. Her promise to Richard resounded in her head, conflicting so violently with temptation to follow her heart, to tell him the truth he maybe needed to hear.

'Does it really matter?' He shook his head, stared at her for a painful second longer. 'I just can't do this, Mia.'

Despite the hot water her body was cold without him. Turning her back, she tried in vain to ignore the image of him peeling off his saturated clothes, wrapping a towel around that divine body, only remembering to breathe again when finally the door closed behind him and she was left alone. Shivering under the water, she stood there, knowing it could never be over, knowing that in a few moments she'd be facing him again.

And wondering how she could do it.

How she could look him in the eye and somehow not reveal the secret truth that only Mia now knew.

CHAPTER FIVE

IT WAS a very different Ethan that greeted Mia as hesitantly she joined him on the patio. To date Mia had only seen him wearing a suit or the best part of nothing at all, but dressed in denim jeans, so dark they were almost navy, topped with a black jumper, his hair flopping over his forehead as it quickly dried in the hot midday sun, Ethan Carvelle for the first time since yesterday bordered on approachable.

And it wasn't just his rather more informal attire.

The contempt had gone from the eyes that greeted hers as she shyly sat down. Dressed in a pair of Ethan's boxers and a massive oversize T-shirt he had thoughtfully left on her bed.

'Thanks for these.' She pulled at the baggy white top. 'I think my bump's expanded even since yesterday. I didn't much fancy struggling into that black dress again.'

Another long silence ensued, but this time it wasn't uncomfortable, just a quiet pause as Ethan filled two long glasses with fruit juice and pushed a plate of pastries towards her.

'No, thanks…' Mia started, then checked herself, remembering their conversation last night, instead reluctantly selecting a chocolate croissant and not feeling quite so hard done by as she bit into the sweet dough, the bitter chocolate a delectable contrast.

'Nice?' Ethan asked.

'Very. You'll have to tell me where you got them, so I can take a stack back with me when I go home. Fattening myself up might not be so hard after all!'

His eyes narrowed for a moment, but he didn't rise, just took a long drink before finally he spoke.

'Can we talk, Mia? I mean, can we try and have a conversation without arguing?'

'I doubt it.' She gave a small hollow laugh, ran a finger around the rim of her glass before finally screwing her eyes closed and nodding. 'But we can try.'

'I can see how it happened.' He gave a long ragged sigh. 'I can still hear the row in my head. My father was furious the night Richard came back—livid, in fact. He was determined to get to the bottom of things and anyone who's seen my father like that would know that Richard didn't stand a chance against him, would understand why Richard chose to lie.'

'Was it always like that with your parents?' Mia asked, drifting off the subject but desperate for insight. 'Richard just clammed right up whenever I tried to find out about his childhood.'

'With good reason,' Ethan said darkly, his eyes fixing on her then, a question in his voice when he spoke, only this time his words weren't derogatory. 'Mia, if Richard had lived, would you still have raised the baby alone?'

She gave a small hesitant nod. 'We'd decided that Richard would be involved, would play a big part in our child's life, but I was always going to be the sole carer.'

'Sole carer?' A slightly patronizing note tinged his words and Mia fought quickly back.

'I thought we were going to attempt to get through this conversation without a row, Ethan. If that can only happen if I say what you want to hear, then we might as well call it a day here and now.'

'I'm sorry.' He put up his hand. 'I really am. In fact, I have no right to judge you, Mia. For some strange reason I've always held this ingrained belief that two parents are better than one—' She went to stand, to terminate this discussion. Ethan didn't have to agree with her, but his disparaging remarks she could well do without. But he caught her hand, asked her to sit with his eyes and after a moment's hesitation Mia complied.

'If you'll let me finish, I was about to say that, given my upbringing, it's a rather strange belief to hold. You'll be a wonderful mother, Mia.' He watched the colour suffuse her cheeks before continuing. 'I'd give anything for your baby's one parent to my own two!' He let out a long sigh. 'I'm not surprised in the least that Richard clammed up when he spoke about his childhood. My parents are two of the coldest people you could ever meet and, if that sounds a bit over the top, believe me, I'm not exaggerating.

It amazes me that they even had sex once let alone twice…'

'You don't have sex just to get pregnant.' Mia's lips bordered on an ironic smile, but it faded when she registered the flash of pain in his eyes.

'Not one kiss, not one cuddle.' His voice was bland, without a trace of self-pity, but Mia's heart bled for him. 'Nanny after nanny was paraded in front of us, but as soon as we got to know their names, no sooner had they found out how we liked our eggs in the morning, our parents assumed we were becoming "too attached" and they were replaced. It was a relief finally to go to boarding-school.'

'So why did they have children?' Mia asked. 'When it sounds as if they didn't even want them around?'

'They didn't want children.' Ethan's eyes held hers and if she'd witnessed pain before it was nothing compared to the despair behind his words. 'They wanted heirs. That's all we were, and when it was clear Richard wasn't going to come around, when it was clear that he wasn't going to come back and assume what our parents decreed was his rightful role in the family hotel business, he was cut off with barely a backwards glance. That's the type of people my parents are, I'm afraid.'

'Yet you work with them,' Mia pointed out. 'You chose to stay.'

He gave a small shrug, but it infuriated her, the shutters coming down, the barriers coming up again.

'Talk to me, Ethan. You're the one who insisted we talk. You can't have it both ways. You can't demand I open up to you and then sit there in judgment. Why did you stay? If they're so awful why do you still work with them? You don't strike me as the subservient kind—'

'I'm not,' Ethan broke in. 'But they gave Richard such hell, were fully prepared to just cut him off...'

'Is that why you stayed?' Looking up, he saw a questioning frown pucker her brow, registered the confusion in her eyes. 'So that they wouldn't cut you off as well?'

'No.' He shook his head slowly, before downing his drink in one gulp. 'Believe me, Mia, I'd have loved to have gone, would have loved to wash my hands of the bloody lot of them.'

'They're your family.' Mia gasped, shocked by the brutality of his words, but Ethan remained unmoved.

'They're my parents,' he said without a trace of affection. 'That's all they are to me, nothing more, nothing less. I stayed working for them so that they'd let Richard go...'

'Please.' She gave a scoffing laugh, but it halted midway, something in his stance telling her she was glimpsing the real man behind the rather austere, scathing version that was usually on show, hearing the painful truth for once, or as close to it as Ethan was likely to reveal.

'Mia, if I'd have walked away that would have been it, it would have been over. I could have sur-

vived,' he said with his usual arrogance. 'Hell, I'd
have excelled. But not Richard.' He shook his head,
his voice low and pensive, more talking to himself
than her now. 'He'd have been like some beautiful
oriental cat, suddenly thrown out with the ferals. He
wouldn't have lasted five minutes out there. When
they moved to Sydney they were totally prepared to
sign him out of their lives.'

'But you stepped in?'

He nodded. 'I made sure Richard at least got a
decent allowance from them right up to the day he
died. He was at least given a chance to go to art
school and follow his dreams, which might seem
more than most people get, but at the end of the day
he is a Carvelle...' he swallowed hard '...was a
Carvelle. If it wasn't for me he'd have been dossing
on the floor of your love shack...'

And if she hadn't heard the raw pain behind his
voice, she'd have snapped back a retort, but instead
she sat quietly, terrified almost to move, to break the
magical spell. And in a mawkish way it *was* magical,
seeing this aloof, distant man actually open up a
touch. 'Mia, you witnessed firsthand how they treated
your father and, as bad as it might have seemed at
the time, believe me, if I hadn't been there it would
have been far worse.'

'In what way?'

'In *every* way. I fought tooth and nail to make sure
your father got a decent pay-out.'

'Hush money, more like,' Mia retorted, but Ethan just shrugged.

'Call it what you like, but he got a damn sight more than he would have if it had been left to my parents. Don't think for a moment they wouldn't have called the police on their own son if they'd found out the truth. Money's their God, Mia. Mere mortals, even their own sons, don't get a look-in. I keep them on the straight and narrow. I'm good at what I do, good enough that they actually need me now, and I'm powerful enough to wield some influence as well—I'm the only person who can talk them down when they go too far.'

'Talent and a social conscience?' She was using his words, lightening the atmosphere a touch, but tears were stinging her eyes as she did so, scarcely able to fathom the cold nature of his family, the lonely, harsh world the Carvelles had created for their children. 'So that's the only reason you stay?'

'Hell, no.' Startled, she blinked back at him, watching as an almost cheeky grin twitched his lips. 'I make a shit-load of money as well.'

'I guess every job has its perks.' Her smile was gratefully received; a tiny moment to regroup before he shifted the conversation.

'Will you tell me now what the doctor said?'

'I pretty much have.' She gave a tight shrug, and maybe it had been a calculated move of Ethan's, maybe it was just another one of his strange mind games, but, given how he'd opened up, Mia felt that the least she could do was reciprocate. 'My blood pressure's still a bit high.'

'Which means?'

'He's not sure yet. He said that I need to be monitored more closely. That, though it would be easy to put the rise in blood pressure down to the stress of the past few weeks, there was also a possibility that…'

'That the baby's in danger?' Ethan asked when Mia didn't finish.

'Both of us could be in danger. The doctor's concerned that I might be in the early stages of toxaemia.' She registered the confusion in his eyes. 'It's a complication of pregnancy. It can cause convulsions…'

'Like Richard had?'

She took a nervous swig of her drink, trying and failing not to picture the convulsions that had racked Richard's frail body in his final few weeks. 'It's only a possibility,' Mia said as dismissively as possible, but she knew she wasn't fooling anyone, least of all Ethan.

'You know you can't go home, Mia,' Ethan said softly, but there was firmness behind every word. 'You can't be alone now.'

'But I can't stay here.' Anxiety was creeping into her voice and she fought to counter it. Emotion crackled in the air around them, sizzled across the table between them, but it had to, *had to* stay out of the conversation. Too much was at stake now to lose her head and say something she would surely regret. 'I can't, Ethan.'

'Because of what happened between us?'

She nodded, the simple truth tearing her apart.

'Would it help if I told you what's happened between us will never be repeated? Would it help if I told you that, as much as I feel for you, Mia, that after this morning I now realize too much has gone on, that there's too much past between us to look to the future?'

'Is that how you really feel?'

'It's Richard's baby.' His voice was hoarse, thick with emotion as he stared at her across the table and he fought for eloquence, tried to rip through the pain and somehow convey that it wasn't just the fact it was Richard's child she was carrying. That fact he could deal with, he was even happy about, thrilled that a part of Richard would live on, that his legacy would continue, that a child would be born with his brother's blood flowing through its veins. It wasn't the baby that was mentally bringing him to his knees, sending his normally well-checked emotions into a furious spin, but the tangible proof that Richard had loved her, that, even though it had been seven years after the assumed event, what he had dreaded most, the one thing he couldn't forgive, had finally happened. 'I just can't pretend...' His voice petered out, words failing him as he stared into those delectable aquamarine pools, saw the sun catch her golden hair, had to clench his fists because if he didn't he'd have reached out to touch her.

'It's okay,' she whispered through pale lips, wishing it didn't have to be so, wishing that the might that Ethan Carvelle supposedly was could be strong enough to love another man's child. 'I can manage on my own.'

'You don't have to be alone,' Ethan countered. 'Just because it can't work out for us, it doesn't mean I can't be there for you, for the baby too.'

'We'll manage,' she responded, but the tremor in her voice was audible even to Mia.

'Stay,' Ethan urged gently. 'At least for the baby's sake. I'll stay out of your way as much as I can, give you your privacy, there will be no repeats of this morning's episode. This really isn't the time to be living alone, Mia, miles away from medical help.'

'I need to work,' Mia argued. 'Ethan, I've got a contract. I've got a painting waiting to be done that I haven't even started; if I don't get the work done before the baby arrives, heaven only knows when I'll be able to complete it.'

'Do you really think you'll be able to work?' Ethan asked perceptively. 'Do you really think, given all that's taken place, you're going to be able to go home and throw yourself into your art?'

'I have to.' Mia gulped, while realizing the futility of her own words. As gentle as Garth had been he had scared her, not for herself, but for the baby. Ethan was right: alone in the mountains was the last place a woman in her condition should be, and the knowledge of that would be enough alone to throw her off her stride, that she couldn't truly immerse herself in her art with the knowledge that her baby was in danger.

'Let me help,' Ethan insisted. 'Look, I know Richard didn't mention the baby in his will, but I'm sure if he'd had more time then it would have been addressed. The details haven't all been finalized, he's got a property that's in the process of being sold, his life insurance policy, I'm sure we can—'

'I don't need Richard's money.' She stared back at him. 'Ethan, this was never about money. As hard as it is for you to understand, money was never my motive.'

'I do believe you, Mia, but be realistic—'

'I am being. Ethan, my business is doing really well. I'm more than capable of supporting myself, I'm paying off my home, the gallery's taking care of itself, I'm more than comfortable.'

'You're still paying off your home?' Shrewd business eyes narrowed. 'Mia I thought you said it was a dump. What about your father's house? Surely that would have covered it.' When she didn't answer he pressed on. 'Or did you keep it as an investment property?'

'I didn't sell it and I didn't keep it.' There was an edge to her voice that had him frowning. 'My dad met someone, he married again…'

'She got to keep the house when he died?' His voice was incredulous.

'Her name is Sally, Ethan, and she didn't *get* to keep the house, she continues to live in the home she shared with my father.'

'But they can't have been married long, for heaven's sake. Surely you should have inherited—'

'I inherited plenty,' Mia broke in. 'My father left me a legacy far greater than money. Sally loved my father and he loved her. Love isn't some mathematical equation: X amount of hours multiplied by X amount of love, Ethan. Sally made my father happy in his final years and for that I'm eternally grateful.'

'But even so…'

'How long does it take to find love, Ethan? Two years, two months—' she gave a hollow laugh '—two weeks? Is the love my father and Sally shared any less real because the years didn't run into double figures?' He didn't answer her question, just stared at her for the longest time.

'Stay,' he said finally, only this time there was no question in his voice. 'I'll drive over to your home this afternoon and pick up your things.'

'What about my work?'

'You can work from here.' He gestured towards the alfresco area. 'It's covered, and there are sliding doors that can be pulled closed in case it rains.'

'Have you any idea the havoc my clay and paint will wreak on your expensive imported tiles?'

'I guess I'm about to find out.' He stared back at

her quizzically, watching her forehead furrow, her eyes crinkling as she weighed up his offer. 'You know this makes sense.'

'It makes no sense.' She flashed a watery smile. 'None of this makes sense, Ethan. I'm supposed to be taking things easy, keeping the baby's world calm and, with the best will in the world, living with you…' She shook her head helplessly, unsure how, even if she had the courage, even if she could some-how wave a magic wand and imbue herself with wanton daring, she would be able to voice how he made her feel. How could she even begin to express how living with him, seeing his haughty, brooding face first thing in the morning and last thing at night and knowing he was out of bounds, knowing that the small intimacy they had shared that morning could never be repeated, never be expanded, wasn't exactly conducive to staying calm? But she didn't need to explain, didn't need to reveal how deeply she felt, because Ethan got there first, pulling the plug on the last drops of hope.

'It's over between us, Mia.' His voice was void of emotion. Eyes that had adored her were distant now, as if someone had turned off a light switch inside, reached and pulled out the passionate heart that had once beat there. 'It was over seven years ago, and in regards to what happened this morning…' He barely paused, didn't even appear uncomfortable, addressing the facts as if he were summing up a meeting. Mia half expected to look over and see a faithful secretary efficiently taking shorthand as Ethan shuffled the mental papers of their encounter, addressed the facts as he saw fit.

'While it's regrettable that it happened, there were of course a number of extenuating circumstances to account for what took place this morning: we were both upset, both still overwhelmed from the previous day's events. Richard's death has hit us both hard.' He stared back at her, presumably expecting a nod of agreement, but moving on anyway as Mia blinked back at him. 'To deny there is an attraction between us would be a lie. Combine that attraction with emotion, add a confined space and the fact you were naked—'

'You should get a projector, Ethan.' She watched him stiffen as she interrupted, a frown puckering his brow as she carried on. 'And a little white stick, or perhaps one of those laser pointers that looks like a pen...'

He gave her a slightly startled look, as if she were some sort of mental patient on day release he'd been lumbered with, someone he had to at least attempt to empathize with no matter how trying. 'What's the problem, Mia?'

'You are,' Mia replied rather rudely. 'Why don't you stand, Ethan? Why don't you go and drag your laptop out here and give me a little impromptu PowerPoint presentation?'

'I've no idea what you're talking about, Mia.'

'I'm talking about you and your bloody extenuating

circumstances!' Mia snapped. 'I'm talking about the way you insist on reducing anything and everything into cold, hard facts, when the fact of the matter is—'

'The fact is this, Mia,' Ethan broke in, and his voice held a warning ring, which despite her fury and bubbling temper Mia heeded. 'This isn't about you and it isn't about me. It's about what's best for the baby.' He let his words sink in, watched as the anger fizzed out of her, replaced instead by a weary sadness as Ethan continued. 'And the best thing for the baby is for you to stay here, near medical help, and, however clumsily and inappropriately I tried to sum things up, the simple truth is that there will be no repeat of this morning. There cannot nor ever will be an *us*. It's as simple as that.'

And it was, or it should have been, but tears pricked her eyes at the finality of it all, a shiver of grief for all she had lost. Ethan was right; it was as simple and as horrible and as awful as that.

Their time had passed.

She felt the baby stir, her hands instinctively massaging the child within, a tiny life that mattered more than hers right now, a little person that deserved the very best she could give.

No matter the personal cost.

And it would be at a cost—seeing Ethan each morning, spending the day with him and knowing she could never have him, that she could almost deal with, but saying goodnight, wandering to her separate room and lying a few feet away from the only man she could ever love would surely be the hardest feat of all.

'Stay for the baby,' Ethan said again, and, though she couldn't bring herself to look at him, Mia nodded. 'Write out a list of what you want me to fetch and I'll head over there this afternoon.'

'I'll come with you.'

'I'll need to hire a truck, Mia.' He gave a half-smile. 'I doubt I'll fit all your art equipment in my car. Anyway, the whole point of this exercise is to keep you near medical help. It kind of defeats the purpose if we head off to the mountains on the first day.'

'I suppose,' Mia admitted. 'I'll go and write a list, but it will be a big one,' she warned. 'If I'm going to work from here you can't miss anything out…'

'I can read,' he responded tartly, which sounded a bit more like the old Ethan. 'And if I can't find some-thing, I can always ring. You do have a phone, I as-sume?'

'No,' Mia replicated his sarcasm. 'But you can al-ways start a bonfire in the garden and send me some smoke signals. I'll watch out for them from the sun lounger.' Standing, she headed for the house, sud-denly desperate to get away, to curl up on her bed and lick her wounds, to mourn the loss of what she had never really had, but before she did, before finally she moved on, there was one last thing she needed to know.

'Can you answer me one thing, Ethan?' Turning,

she expected to face him, but his back was to her, one hand gripping the balcony, the other on his glass as he stared out into the endless ocean, his shoulders rippling with tension beneath the black T-shirt. She ached for him to turn around, to face her, but had to settle for the back of his head when he didn't move. 'If Richard hadn't lied, if he hadn't said what he did, do you think we…?' Her voice trailed off. 'It doesn't matter.' Pulling the door open, she stepped inside, only pausing as Ethan called her back, the ramifications of her loss only truly hitting home as Ethan answered her unspoken question.

'We'd have made it, Mia.'

He turned around to face her, and for the longest time she stood there, and what he had expected from his answer he truly didn't know—regret, sadness, a tired smile—but her response knocked the breath from him. With her tiny defiant chin jutting proudly, her earrings sparkling in the sunlight, she shook her head slowly.

'Then more fool you, Ethan.'

CHAPTER SIX

MORE fool you, Ethan.

The words resounded in his head like a broken record, playing over and over as he shifted the gears along the long winding road. The thundering noise of the rental truck should have been enough to blow the lingering thoughts away, but nothing could drown out the mantra, nothing could erase the hint of pity in Mia's voice as he replayed the words.

A hand-painted sign had his foot slamming on the brakes. He berated himself for his lack of attention as he skilfully reversed the vehicle, before indicating right and turning into a gravelly unsealed road.

'Mia's Home!'

'Mia's home indeed,' he muttered to himself, cursing Mia for her stupid, trusting nature. He was tempted to rip the shoddy sign down himself, to snap the gnarled wood over his knee and toss it into the massive ferns that shaded the driveway. 'Why not just write single woman living alone?' He swore to himself, pulling on the handbrake and jumping down, ripping the sign out of the mulch in one motion and throwing it into the passenger seat beside him, driving up the steep entrance, bracing himself for what he didn't know, blinking in disbelief as he ground the truck to a halt.

It was beautiful.

A massive old Queenslander home, high on stilts, standing tall and proud in the mountain, a million miles from the tinpot shack he had mentally relegated her to. Not a struggling artist in sight, not even a rabid-looking cat searching for scraps as he slowly mounted the front stairs, pulling open the fly screen and slowly turning the key in the door.

And even though she knew he was there, and it was with her consent, he felt as if he were invading, felt almost voyeuristic as his eyes wandered around the building—her house, her *home*, so overtly feminine, every surface brimming with Mia, every cushion, every fluttering net that danced in the windows an extension of the woman he knew—glimpsing into the world of the woman he had pushed away all those years ago. Her lingering scent filled his nostrils and he inhaled deeply, a scent so evocative, so elusive he had chased it for seven years. A lingering waft as he walked through a department store was enough to stop him literally in his tracks, the mere scent of it on another woman enough to…

He closed his eyes in tormented regret.

Shame, self-loathing even, imbued him as he recalled the nameless faces on the pillows he had awoken to over the years, and he knew in one dreadful moment of introspection what he had been searching for all those long, lonely nights. The gaping void in his life he had tried desperately to fill even on a temporary basis, an attempt to bury the pain just a bit deeper, to hold and be held the way he had been once before, and always to no avail. Like sitting down to a five-course meal just to get to the dessert—the endless chatter irritating, the feel of another woman that wasn't Mia in his arms disappointing at times, devastating at others.

So what the hell was he doing now? Ethan thought darkly to himself, wandering from room to room. What was he doing fuelling the need instead of dousing it? Dragging himself in deeper when he should be pulling away? Entwining himself further into her life when he should be cutting himself free?

His eyes fixed on a photo of his brother and the image stilled him, pale blue eyes staring back at him, one arm thrown casually around Mia, smiles on their faces yet not a trace of love in sight.

He didn't understand.

Reaching into his pocket, he pulled out his wallet, stared at the faded photo he had carried for seven years, the photo he had gone back to collect from the restaurant where they'd first met before he'd left for Sydney.

After his world had fallen apart.

As he stared at their images, so much younger, so much more carefree than they were now, he could almost feel the crackling tension that had surrounded them that night, see the giddy lust in their eyes, feel the unrelenting need that had danced between them.

'Mia.' He said it out loud, could feel her so close he half expected a response, half expected her to walk from the bedroom, that subtle smile on her face, a questioning look in those kitten eyes at the surprising softness in his voice. Shaking his head fiercely, he shoved the wallet back in his pocket, slammed the lid on dangerous thoughts and, pulling out her impressive list, set to work.

There were reprieves.

As the days ticked by into weeks, the agony of being so close, so near, while knowing he was out of bounds, thankfully wasn't constant.

The occasional, blissful interlude from her self-imposed torture made the pain more bearable. Tiny snatches of laughter broke the strained silences every now and then and as the hours ticked into days, as the days slipped into weeks, every now and then, lying by the pool, feeling the bliss of the sun on her swollen stomach, exposed with her T-shirt knotted above it, lying with eyes closed, semi dozing as Ethan tapped away on his computer on the other side of the pool, Mia was almost at peace with the world. Able to drift off, to focus on the baby, or not, as the case might be, to just drift and, if not forget, push aside the wretchedness of unrequited love.

'Here.'

Opening her eyes, she found it impossible to focus for a moment, and Ethan waited patiently as she scrabbled for her sunglasses, sitting up in the sun lounger and trying to pretend that she hadn't been asleep again. Passing her a glass of something icy, he stood for a moment as she took a sip, then, almost tentatively, perched himself on the edge of the sun lounger.

'I thought you should have a drink and put some sun screen on. It's not good to fall asleep in the sun.'

'I wasn't asleep.' As she registered his disbelieving look her voice was more insistent. 'I wasn't! Actually I was lying here and thinking about the work I'm going to do this afternoon.'

'Really?'

'I am,' Mia insisted, instantly jumping to the defence at his rather loaded word. She was painfully aware that since he'd headed for the hills, dragged her equipment all the way back and spent the best part of two days setting it up for her she hadn't so much as picked up a brush. 'Art doesn't just happen, Ethan. As chaotic as my work might look to you, it actually takes a lot of planning, so you see I wasn't asleep, just...' she struggled for a second '...developing an idea,' Mia finished with a note of triumph, happy with her choice of words.

Even Ethan looked suitably impressed.

'So tell me, Mia. Do you always dribble when you develop an idea?'

She should have blushed, thumped him, died of shame, but instead she laughed, laughed so much it almost hurt until even Ethan finally joined in.

'You're getting some colour,' Ethan said and the laughter faded, replaced with a falsely bright smile as his eyes flicked over her body. 'You were way too pale before.'

Before.

Before Ethan stepped back into her life.

Before Ethan turned her world around with a crook of his manicured finger.

'I didn't exactly have much time for sun baking.'

He nodded but didn't say anything and it was Mia who elaborated.

'It wasn't just visiting Richard that took up my time. I tend to get engrossed in my work. When I disappear into my studio, when I'm really deep into a piece, a whole day can pass without me even stepping outside.'

'I wish my work was that absorbing,' Ethan quipped. 'Believe me, all distractions are gratefully received when you're staring at a pile of figures, trying to fathom ways to woo a few more tourists!'

'I don't believe you for a moment,' Mia answered. 'A bomb could go off and you wouldn't move. I've watched you working...' Her voice petered out; she was cross with herself for revealing too much, but Ethan didn't seem to notice her sudden embarrassment.

'So how come, if it's so absorbing, that you're not working now?' He gestured to the mountain of equipment he'd retrieved from her studio and she eyed it guiltily—every last thing on her list had been accounted for, every last piece of equipment she might possibly need had been set up, all waiting for her to grace it with her presence. He'd even been sweet enough to bring the sign from her driveway, mounted it on the alfresco area in an attempt to make her feel at home. 'I thought you had a deadline looming.'

'I do,' Mia responded, chewing nervously on her bottom lip, wishing Ethan hadn't reminded her of a truth she was trying to ignore, the horribly gnawing knowledge of a deadline looming and not a lot to show for it. 'It's just…'

'Just what?' Ethan asked shrewdly.

'You wouldn't understand.'

'Try me,' Ethan offered, and she shook her head.

'Try me,' he said again and, behind her dark glasses, Mia rolled her eyes, but, even despite her misgivings, she relented, hoping against hope that maybe by voicing her fears out loud she could come to some sort of resolution.

It never entered her head that Ethan might have an answer.

'It's just not happening for me at the moment.'

'Not happening?' When she didn't elaborate he pushed further. 'What exactly is it that's "not happening"?'

'I don't know,' Mia responded stiffly to his obvious bemusement.

'You don't know what's "not happening".'

'See, I knew you wouldn't understand,' Mia retorted, wishing he'd just drop it, but Ethan clearly had other ideas.

'You haven't exactly explained what the problem is. If you're hoping for an objective opinion, then you have to at least arm me with the facts.'

'Here we go again,' Mia muttered quietly, but obviously not quietly enough as Ethan's eyes narrowed. 'Not everything can be relegated to facts, Ethan.

There isn't always an answer. When I say it's not happening I don't actually know what "it" is.' She thought for a moment, realized she wasn't making much sense. 'Inspiration's the word I'm looking for, I suppose. I'm supposed to be doing five small post-card-sized oils for this Japanese—'

'I thought you only sculpted for commission.'

'I paint as well.' Mia whistled through gritted teeth. 'Or at least I'm supposed to be at the moment. The trouble is I have no idea where to start.'

'But surely you've spoken to your client; surely there's some sort of blueprint to work to. Do you know what type of work he wants?'

'Sort of,' Mia mumbled, then righted herself. This was her career, her work. Just because it couldn't be defined to a suit like Ethan didn't mean there was anything to be embarrassed about. Sitting upright, she pulled off her sunglasses and stared him right in the eye. 'Look, Mr Koshomo has pretty much left it to me. He just wants the beauty of the Queensland coast and mountains captured, he wants different angles explored, different glimpses…'

'And have you decided what these "glimpses" will be?'

'Of course.' Mia nodded. 'In fact I've already done four of them. I've only one more to go…' And she waited, waited for Ethan to state the obvious, to say something stupid like, 'Well, paint it, then,' but thankfully he didn't. He just stared back at her till it was Mia who finally dropped her eyes, even managing a wobbly smile as Ethan finally spoke.

'So given the fact you're not actually painting, that instead you're lying here sleeping.' He grinned as she winced. 'Sorry, I mean *developing your idea*, that what you're actually suffering from is…' for the first time he struggled to find the words '…artist's block.'

'I suppose I am,' Mia answered tartly. 'And suffering is the word, believe me.' She gave him an apologetic shrug, realizing however pompous, however arrogant Ethan could be at times her anger was for once misdirected. This really wasn't Ethan's fault. 'Look, thanks for listening, thanks for trying to understand, but the simple fact is, Ethan, that there's nothing you can do to help me. I've just got to wait, hopefully patiently, till…'

'*It* happens?' Ethan asked, and Mia actually smiled at the impossible thought of Ethan Carvelle attempting to understand something that couldn't be defined, or added, divided and subtracted till it fitted that mould.

Something that simply *was*.

'Tell me when it does.'

'Believe me, you'll know.'

He was still staring, embarrassing her with his scrutiny, and, even though they were outside, suddenly she felt impossibly claustrophobic, desperate for space, for distance.

'I'm going for a walk.' She stood up, swinging her legs on the other side of the sun lounger, slipping on her sandals and heading purposefully back to the house.

'In this heat?' Ethan was right behind her, and her

step quickened. She was desperate to shake him off, annoyed at herself for already revealing too much, for allowing Ethan to see a weak link, knowing he would exploit it in an instant, ram home yet again the appalling insecurity of an artist's living, force her to question again how she could possibly hope to raise a child. 'But it's nearly lunchtime—anyway, it's hardly the weather for an afternoon stroll.'

'Then I'll go somewhere cool.' Mia gave an irritated shrug. 'I'll take a picnic perhaps. There's a nice rainforest nearby…' She nodded then, pleased at her decision, glad of the temporary reprieve she had given herself: a few hours away from Ethan, a few hours out of this cauldron of emotion. She could lose herself for a while in the forest, get out of the stifling heat Ethan created with his mere presence.

'Sounds good.'

'What are you doing?' Appalled, she stared at him, watching with mounting horror as he pulled open the fridge.

'Preparing lunch, although…' he eyed the contents of the refrigerator '…there are not exactly the tools here for an impromptu picnic. I'll ring the deli, have them pack us a basket. We can collect it on the way.'

'We?'

'Of course.' He gave her that slightly incredulous look he used on occasion. 'You weren't thinking of wandering off on your own were you, in your condition?'

'Pregnant women do walk, Ethan. I'm not completely helpless.'

'I never said you were.' He gave a slightly patronizing smile. 'But most heavily pregnant women don't go wandering around rainforests alone—not the local ones, anyway. They'd know there's no hope of picking up a phone signal; they'd know that, even though it looks beautiful and safe, in fact it's quite a climb to get there. And unless you fancy a trip in a helicopter courtesy of the local rescue squad I'd suggest you go and put on some decent footwear.' Picking up the phone, he flashed a triumphant smile as Mia stood there open-mouthed. 'How does mango chicken sound?'

'Mango chicken?'

'For the salad?'

He didn't even await her response, just barked his orders into the phone as she marched off into the bedroom and got ready, returning a moment later, bristling with indignation as Ethan stood tapping his foot at the door. 'Come on, Mia, I thought you'd at least be dressed by now?'

A tiny smile of triumph edged on the corner of her mouth. 'But I am dressed.'

She watched him swallow, watched as he deliberately tried and failed not to look shocked, his mouth disappearing as he stared at her ripe stomach barely concealed by a flimsy lilac organza top, her slender legs fully revealed in the shortest of denim shorts.

'Of course, had you packed my navy elasticated trousers and my white smock topped with a neatly tied royal blue bow, I'd be more suitably dressed...'

'It wasn't on the list,' Ethan croaked, her sarcasm

clearly wasted on him as, not quite so assertive now, he followed her out the door. 'I'm sure you didn't put it on the list.'

Instantly it soothed her.

A half-hour winding trip, stopping at the deli *en route*, even if it was in a luxury air-conditioned car, had done nothing to improve her temper, nothing to ease the knot of tension Ethan created by his mere presence, but a few metres into the bosky dampness of the tiny virgin rainforest and Mia felt the tension seep out of her. She breathed deeply on the damp air, the sweet scent of fern, heard the distant constant gush of a waterfall and she felt herself relax, perhaps for the first time since she had lain eyes on Ethan at the church. The harsh Australian sun was a distant memory in this divine oasis, its unrelenting glare trapped in the tall green canopy the leaves created, the mulch damp beneath the feet, barely making a sound as they walked idly along the winding paths, stopping every now and then as a distant bird screeched. Even though it was a tiny forest, they might as well have been in the Amazon, endless hues of green, chirping insects, screeching birds filling their senses at every turn.

'I love it here.' Arching her head backwards, she stared upwards, ever upwards, to the hidden tips of the giant Kauri trees, climbing ever taller as they reached for the sun, enjoying her insignificance against this beautiful, majestic work of art.

'This one's over a thousand years old.' Ethan

stepped over the knotted roots and stroked the solid trunk before turning round and smiling at her startled expression. 'I came here with school. We were doing a project on the ecosystem of a rainforest; I made a mini model of it and if I remember rightly got top marks, not that it impressed my parents— ''What the hell has nature got to do with anything?'' '

'They said that?'

'Words to that effect.' She sensed a sudden pensive shift, realized she had hit a nerve and moved quickly to change the subject, aching for the closeness they had briefly shared in that moment to be retrieved.

'*You* were a schoolboy?'

For the first time he smiled, really smiled, not mocking, no malice, no suspicion in those brooding eyes, just a genuine smile, a tiny shared joke, and the ecosystem of the rainforest must have registered a monumental blip because suddenly the temperature was soaring, Mia's cheeks flaming as Ethan walked back towards her.

'I just can't imagine you cluttering up the dining-room table with bits of fern and Plasticine, *creating* your project.'

'I didn't,' Ethan clipped. 'I made it in the art room at school.'

Mentally Mia kicked herself at her own insensitivity. 'I'm sorry.' Her hand brushed his arm as he started to walk on. 'That was thoughtless of me; I forgot you were at boarding-school.'

'Don't apologize.' He turned and gave a tight smile. 'And, please, don't waste your time feeling sorry for me.' He was walking faster now, the only indication he wasn't as comfortable with the subject as he'd appeared, for the first time since they'd arrived at the rainforest, forgetting she was in fact heavily pregnant, and Mia struggled to keep up with him. 'Believe me, Mia, I wasn't one of those children clinging onto their mothers' dresses at the beginning of term and crying that I didn't want to go back.

'Sorry, remind me if I go too fast.' He paused for a moment as she got her breath back, resuming the conversation where he had left it. 'In fact, it was the other way around—I couldn't wait to go back, couldn't wait for the first day of term; I was one of the few kids who actually dreaded the holidays.'

He said it in a completely matter-of-fact voice, with that flippant edge that Mia knew so well, but the lonely image it created in her mind brought a sting of tears to her eyes, which she rapidly blinked back, knowing her sympathy was neither wanted nor needed. 'I loved doing that project...' His voice was suddenly wistful, the words spoken in such low tones Mia almost missed them. 'I had the last laugh, though!'

'How?'

'It's all about nature now, up here in Queensland anyway. You can't cough without considering the effect it will have on the environment, let alone build a resort. That little project came in very useful, as it turned out.'

'I never pictured you as environmentally friendly.'

She gave a small, slightly nervous laugh. 'You're not even particularly *friendly*.'

'Oh, I can be.' He turned to face her then, and, whether it was there or not, he pushed a tendril of hair off her face, smiling into her eyes. 'Given the right circumstances.' Suddenly he seemed aware of the intimacy he had initiated, dropping his hand and looking around, leaving Mia dizzy and confused, his mere touch, the sudden glimpse of closeness tipping her back into dangerous waters, stirring memories definitely better forgotten. 'We came for the day. I remember crossing a bridge...' His eyes narrowed, scanning the forest, searching for a landmark. 'I think it was that way...'

'It is.' She walked on purposefully. 'How long is it since you've been here?'

'Twenty years.'

It was Mia stopping in her tracks now as Ethan marched on. 'You've never been back.'

'Never.' He gave a tight shrug. 'Which is pretty poor, given that I own it. Careful, now,' he barked as she stumbled.

'You own it?' She shook her head in bewilderment. 'How can you possibly own a rainforest?'

'I'll show you the deeds,' he responded easily. 'So, it would seem you've been trespassing all these years, Mia. This land is mine right down to where it meets the white beaches of the Coral Sea—at least that's what the brochure the estate agent sent me said. I bought it for a song a few years back with an idea to build a resort...'

'Surely not,' Mia wailed. 'You'd ruin it.'

'Probably,' Ethan admitted. 'Although done properly…' He paused for a moment, and so did Mia, taking in the beauty, the haven that Mother Nature had created. 'Of course you wouldn't have the resort here—'

'I'd hope not,' Mia interrupted. 'Ethan it's a preposterous idea. How can you even contemplate ripping into this land?'

'I'm not,' he answered irritably. 'You don't have to be a lentil-eating hippy to appreciate beauty, you know.'

'I hate lentils,' Mia retorted, but Ethan just laughed.

'You know exactly what I mean. Just because I don't go around waving the peace sign and refusing to wear deodorant, it doesn't mean that I'm a complete philistine when it comes to the environment. It would just be nice to share it with—'

'Rubbish,' Mia broke in. 'You just see it as an easy way to make one hell of a lot of money—no doubt you'd build a few rickety tree-houses, throw in some cane furniture and charge a fortune for the privilege!'

'And I thought I was the cynical one.' He gave a nonchalant shrug. 'Think what you like, Mia, but the fact of the matter is, I make a fortune anyway. I don't need to build another hotel, not in this location anyway. I just had a vision, I guess…' He gave a dry smile. 'I guess I had a flash of the elusive "it" you were going on about.'

'Really?' She blinked up at him, surprised yet curiously pleased all the same at this glimpse of another side to him. 'So what did you envisage?'

He paused and for a moment she didn't think he was going to answer, braced herself for some acid reply, but instead he gazed around. His voice, when finally it came, was slow and pensive, every last word measured, as if he'd really given it some thought.

'The resort would be near the beach, one level only, backing onto the rainforest. But when I say resort, I mean more of a retreat, a place to come and get away, really get away from everything. No boat trips out to the reef, no helicopter pads nearby—there's enough of them. This would just be a place to get away, a place to wander…'

'It sounds wonderful.' Mia sighed, dropping her protest in an instant, seeing his vision with her own eyes. 'So why don't you do it?'

He gave a low laugh. 'Because no matter how I do the sums I can't justify it.'

'Money?' She grinned and Ethan nodded.

'And time. It would really have to be a labour of love to do it right. Maybe one day.' Again she felt as if he were talking to himself more than her. 'Maybe I should just bite the bullet; now Richard's…' His voice trailed off but Mia stepped in, following his thought process, determined that he see it through, at least for a moment.

'Now Richard's gone, there's no need to stay in the family business. You don't have to look out for him any more, Ethan.'

'And I was looking out for him, Mia. I know it was only money I was able to provide…'

'Like it or not, everyone needs it,' she said softly and he gave a slow nod. 'You let Richard follow his own path, Ethan. Now maybe it is time to chase your own dreams.'

They were stepping onto the small suspension bridge, Ethan carrying the heavy basket the deli had prepared and still managing to hold her elbow as she picked her way across the slats, holding onto the rope. Though she'd done it a hundred, maybe a thousand times to date, she realized there and then that Ethan had been right to come, that this really was no place for a pregnant woman to come alone. She felt a thud of disappointment in her chest, a contrast to the shrill ringing in her ears of a warning bell, the mocking taunt that yet again she'd misread the signs, that Ethan's presence had nothing to do with a burning desire to be with her, but a primal need to protect his own, and, whichever way she looked at it, the child within her was part of Ethan, the child within her had Carvelle blood running through its veins and he would do anything to protect it.

'How about this spot?' He took her distracted nod as a yes, spread a rug and gratefully she lowered herself, taking a moment or two to get her breath back.

'Here.' He passed her a bottle of sparkling water and Mia took a long, cool drink, grateful to be waited on, watching as Ethan pulled off lids, spooning delicacies onto a plate before handing it to her. 'You should paint this.' His hand gestured to the magnificent scenery. 'Mr Koshomo would surely be impressed.'

'I already have.' Mia sighed. 'I came here a few months ago. In fact this was the first one in the collection I did. Actually I sat over there.' She motioned to a small clearing. 'Early evening, as the sun gets low it hits the top of the trees. There's an almost golden tinge to the forest that's really quite beautiful...'

He was listening, sort of, but far more magical an image was springing to his mind, the picture of her with a tiny easel, sitting alone with nature. In his mind he could almost see the intense concentration in those azure eyes, that delicious pink tongue bobbing out on her lips as she worked diligently on, and suddenly he was hit in the groin with longing, hollowed out with a lust so tangible he couldn't believe she couldn't sense it, couldn't feel it, couldn't be aware of the sudden shift in his mood.

'I'm boring you,' Mia said apologetically as he rolled onto his stomach, staring somewhere beyond her shoulder with an expression she couldn't read in his eyes.

'So there's only one more painting to go.'

'Just the one.' Her hand was idly fiddling with the ground, scooping the soft mulch into tiny peaks, unearthing the ferny scent as Ethan patiently waited for her to continue. 'It's an underwater one, the reef. I can almost see it in my mind's eye. I know I should just get on and do it, I know that once I start it will probably come...' She shook her head, but her impatience was clearly at herself. 'Sorry to go on about it.'

'Talk to me,' he offered again. 'It might help.'

'It won't.' Mia sunk back on the soft forest floor, stared up at the canopied sky, and it was a purposeful move. She was not wanting to look at him, not wanting Ethan to see the real panic that was surely in her eyes, hear the tremble in her voice as she articulated the fears that had been sniping at her heels for weeks now, the gnawing terror that kept her awake at night.

'Then let's walk.' He was picking up the containers now, tugging at the rug and, though Mia was grateful for the change in subject, grateful to him for realizing she just didn't want to talk about it any more, she wasn't quite ready to move on just yet.

'Let's rest,' she said softly, eyes semi closed, sinking back further onto the soft blanket of the mulch, smiling at the dart of confusion in his eyes as he rather awkwardly replaced the rug and sat woodenly down.

'Rest?'

'Doze.' Mia smiled dreamily, great waves of sleep washing over her.

'But it's four p.m.'

'Don't you ever switch off?' she murmured. 'Just rest for the sake of it?'

'Not in the middle of the day.'

'Try,' she said simply, closing her eyes and breathing deeply, inhaling the delicious scents, the gush of the waterfall the perfect background noise, feeling him rigid and awkward beside her as he tentatively lay down. But, slowly, as the sun dipped lower she heard his breathing wind down, felt the tension seep out from him and, smiling to herself, Mia decided she was probably the first woman in living history to find the low, tiny drones of a man snoring vaguely sexy.

'I've been thinking,' Ethan started hours later as she pretended to stare at the television screen. For something to do Mia had made some popcorn, which of course Ethan had promptly declared he couldn't stand and stalked off to have a shower. So now she sat feeling bloated and ugly on the sofa, with Ethan sitting next to her, smelling divine, nothing on except a dark pair of boxers, long, muscular legs lounging on the coffee-table, crossed at the ankle, the dark hairs on his thigh, still damp from the shower, making tiny curls that she longed to reach out and touch, with the horrible prospect of yet another awkward goodnight looming its ugly head. 'Maybe you need a day off.'

'That's the last thing I need.' Mia sighed, not even turning to face him, just pretending to concentrate on the movie, her hand idly straying to the bowl, then pulling away when she guiltily remembered she'd already eaten the lot. 'I've had more than enough days off recently.'

'I mean a day out.' She could feel his eyes on her, knew Ethan had turned to face her, and she stared fixedly ahead, embarrassed at his scrutiny, trying to feign disinterest as Ethan spoke on. 'Maybe you need to be a tourist for a day! We could go out, pretend to be visitors.'

'What could that possibly achieve? Ethan, I've lived here all my life. I know the ocean, the bay, the cafés. I know every nook and cranny and a day sight-seeing isn't going to change anything.'

'It was just an idea.' Ethan shrugged. 'Sorry for interfering. You're the great artist, you just get on with it.' Still his eyes were on hers and Mia could feel her skin darken, every breath an effort as he stared on, acutely aware of every movement she made, even swallowing a feat in itself. 'Maybe you can lie on the sun lounger all day tomorrow as well and ''develop'' your ideas, you obviously know what you're doing. I'm sure it will all come good in the end.'

The movie was over—at least, the credits were rolling, so Mia *assumed* the movie was over. She'd barely taken in a word of the whole film, so acutely aware of Ethan next to her on the sofa.

'I think I'll have a nightcap. That supposed *doze* went on for two hours…'

'You must have needed it.'

'I need this,' Ethan quipped, pulling himself far more gracefully off the sofa than Mia could even dream of doing in her condition, and poured himself an extremely generous brandy. 'I'll never sleep otherwise. Do you want anything?

'What?' he asked when Mia sucked her breath in in irritation. 'What have I said wrong now?'

'Nothing,' Mia sighed, heaving herself up and padding to the kitchen. A glass of milk was the last thing she wanted, but it was all she could have. A massive brandy would be perfect right now, maybe help her sleep, because there wasn't a chance in hell of getting any shut-eye tonight and it had nothing to do with the fact she'd been dozing all day and everything to do with Ethan. As she walked back into the living room her breath caught as it always did, the mere sight of the back of his head enough to literally stop her in her tracks.

And she couldn't do it.

Couldn't sit on that sofa a moment longer with Ethan beside her and not touch him.

Couldn't listen to the late-night news without creating a scandal of her own, so instead she stood. He was still staring at the screen, the weather girl cheerfully predicting yet another scorching day tomorrow, so vibrant and chirpy it was almost nauseating; such an utter contrast to the loaded atmosphere in the room.

'What did you have in mind?' She saw his head turn slightly at the sound of her voice, glad, eternally glad, that he couldn't see her face as she spoke. 'I mean, when you said we could go out?'

'On a boat. Not mine,' he added, as if it should be a natural assumption that every man and his dog had a huge yacht moored somewhere, 'but a tourist one, like the glass-bottomed one that leaves the pier every morning at eight. It's supposed to be good. They take you over to Lizard Island. We could do a bit of snorkelling…' His voice trailed off and she watched as he gave a tight shrug at her lack of response. 'I asked the doctor about it.' Still he didn't turn fully around to look at her, but he must have sensed her frown. 'I wasn't invading your precious privacy; I thought I'd better run it by him before I suggested anything to you.'

'And what did Garth say?'

'That there shouldn't be a problem—in fact he thought it would do you the world of good. Your blood pressure's down, you're putting on weight; he said that there's no reason why you shouldn't have a day out. The reef's only a forty-five-minute boat ride from here, though Garth did say it might be better to go on an organized tour rather than just the two of us out there alone.

'It was just an idea.'

Silence hung in the air, and Mia felt as if she were balancing on a cliff edge, the relative safety of Ethan's home the haven behind her, Ethan's tempting offer the treacherous drop below.

And it would be a treacherous step, Mia knew that deep down. As casual as his invitation sounded, it was fraught with danger. She had sensed a shift in his mood since the rainforest. The sexual tension that had simmered along these past few weeks seemed to have escalated out of control in the last few hours, a heightened awareness of each other's presence, the pressure cooker of emotions they had somehow kept in check since her first morning in Ethan's home starting to escape now with an ominous hiss. Mia knew, knew as surely as she was standing here now, that if she took this dangerous step the shaky ground they were standing on would crumble beneath them, hurtle them into the unknown, and neither would be left standing.

So why then was she taking a deep breath? Mia wondered. Why was she nodding into the darkness, then opening her mouth to speak?

'It sounds wonderful.'

Her voice was high and slightly breathless and he didn't turn around; her response, quite simply, merited more, so instead he stood, crossing the room and standing in front of her. 'When?'

She could smell him again, feel his closeness invading her personal space, crossing a million unspoken lines with one piercing stare. It would have been so easy to tumble one step further, to fall into the arms she knew would catch her, knew would save her, but without a shadow of doubt Mia knew in the cold, refreshing sensibility of morning light those same arms would push her away again, that the passion, the tension that simmered through the day and became unbearable at night would disperse once again. But right now the tension in the air was so thick it clogged her throat, filled her lungs, every breath dragging that male scent deeper, making it impossible to think straight, impossible to fathom a reason why she shouldn't just take that final step.

'When?' he asked again.

'Whenever.' Her voice was curiously high, she was flinching yet yielding as one hand came up to her face, the bulb of his thumb making contact with the soft flesh of her upper lip.

'You've got a milk moustache.'

Maybe she had one, maybe he was lying, but the contact was unbearable, a rippling effect churning within. Even when his hand moved away, even with the devastation of impact seemingly over, a mushroom cloud of emotion welled within her, the still waters of desire she had put on hold running deeper now, building ominously as he stood a mere breath away.

'I've booked us on for tomorrow.'

She should have argued, should have chided his presumption, his arrogance that he just assumed she would accept…

But it was easier to flee.

To slip between the icy white cotton, to rest her flaming cheeks against the pillow, to close her eyes and push those thoughts away, to ignore her nipples prickling like thistles against the sheet and the relentless throbbing pulse between her thighs, to ignore the daunting implications of his mere touch and just close her eyes and pray for the fresh perspective of morning.

CHAPTER SEVEN

'WELL?'

Staring through the glass-bottomed boat, the coral reef swirling beneath her, fish gliding at her feet as if she were sitting on some massive flat-screen TV, Mia felt her irritation rise and she actually welcomed it.

Welcomed the fact that love wasn't blind.

That Ethan wasn't a man she could love blindly, that the perfect mould she thought he had slipped from did in fact have a few air bubbles and impatience was the one she would love to pop first. 'Well what, Ethan?' He was parked on a tiny wooden bench beside her, thighs involuntary touching courtesy of fifty eager tourists all clamouring for a view. 'You really think it's that easy, don't you? That forty-five minutes of bumping along in a boat and suddenly I'd be inspired.'

He gave a tight shrug, clearly bored already, and Mia sighed, resisting the urge to glance at her watch that wouldn't even be nudging to nine a.m., willing the next eight hours to pass, to get her back to the relative safety of what was slowly becoming home. It had been a stupid idea to come. Oh, not on a professional level—Ethan had been right, damn him. Already, listening to the excited chatter of the tourists, feeling wind whipping around her hair, watching the sun glistening off the ocean, the trail of surf the boat created as it zipped through the glass water, all were serving their purpose, stirring the creative beast within. The grey tinges that had darkened her mental palette these past weeks were already taking on brighter tones, the sapphire of the sky, the emerald of the water, the salty taste on her lips and the sting on her cheeks as the sun kissed them, as if she were seeing it all for the first time, *feeling* it for the first time. But it wasn't only the creative beast that was stirring. Her feeling hadn't abated since last night one iota; the occasional brush of his thigh as the boat lurched sideways, the feel of the hair on his legs dusting across her bare skin like a static charge ricocheting through her, her whole body on high alert, awoken and aware…

'We stop soon.' Ethan yawned, not even bothering to smother it with his hand, seemingly utterly oblivious to the volatile, writhing mass of hormones sitting next to him. 'Maybe once we've had a swim…'

'Excuse me?' Her words were drowned out by the engine, but something in her furious motion caught Ethan's attention. 'There is no way I'm swimming.' She shook her head. 'Ethan, I'm nearly eight months pregnant, for goodness' sake. I'm hardly dressed for swimming…'

'Don't worry about that.' Not remotely perturbed by her outburst, he rummaged in the most expensive-looking backpack Mia had ever seen and pulled out two vaguely familiar pieces of hot red Lycra. 'I packed this for you.'

'This?' Cheeks flaming, Mia grabbed the red rags like an angry bull. 'This is what I wore a year ago when I was thin and gorgeous and had a flat stomach, and it most certainly wasn't on the list I gave you of things to collect.'

'Suit yourself.' The engine was stilling, the excited chatter of the tourists growing louder as Ethan pulled off his T-shirt and in one lithe movement kicked off his runners and dropped his shorts. 'But I for one intend to work up an appetite for the smorgasbord with my complimentary glass of wine.'

'I'm pregnant, Ethan!' Mia shouted as he fiddled with his snorkel mask.

'An extra glass of wine for me, then.' And, as if he'd been in training for the Olympics, he back-flipped over the edge of the boat, leaving her in the sweltering heat, coming up for air with a smile that was purely lethal.

'Don't tell me,' she moaned. 'The water's cool?'

'Actually, no, it's like a bath.'

His eyes were like dark glass, his smile more devastating than she had ever seen it.

'You realize I run the risk of being harpooned if I swim in this!' She held up the offending *almost a* garment.

'Of course you won't be: we're wildlife friendly here in Queensland.' Ethan grinned. 'Or at least according to the multitude of stickers on your awful bomb of a car! Are you coming in?'

She didn't answer, just swallowed back pride as temptation took over and darted into the tiniest loo

Mia had ever seen, undoubtedly collecting a few splinters in her bottom from the wooden walls as she pulled on the hateful bikini. Her only saving grace was the fact she'd shaved her legs that morning, but it didn't stop Mia from blushing furiously and feeling as fat and sexless as a woman could as she climbed down the side ladder of the boat. Ethan's merciless hands guided her into the clear blue water, the scorching red on her cheeks nothing to do with her shame now and everything to do with the familiar hands holding her. She was sure a hiss of steam would surely emanate as she finally submerged herself...

'You have a choice.' Holding what used to be her waist, Ethan stared at her. 'We can either be back on the boat in an hour or we can give the crowds the flick and head over to the island. There's a small resort there, we can get something to eat—'

'Dressed like this?'

'I'm sure they can rustle up a picnic for us if you prefer.' He gave a shrug, but it was anything but nonchalant. 'It was so nice yesterday I figured it might be worth repeating.' His hands were still on her waist, absolutely steady, yet causing more internal motion than her furiously pummelling legs, his eyes in the bright sunlight not black now, but a deep indigo blue. Mia was torn between fear and lust, sorely tempted to flee back to the lonely safety of boat, but fatefully tempted to stay, to spend some time with a man who had declared himself out of bounds, to drink just a little from the forbidden cup he seemed to be offering, to tease herself just a little while longer with what she

could never have. 'A picnic sounds nice.' Her tongue
bobbed out, moistened her full lips, his hands still a
solid presence around her, her voice a mere croak as
she carried on talking. 'You'll have to go back, let
the captain know…'

'I already did.'

He was gone before she could scold him, pulling
on his mask and duck-diving down barely leaving a
ripple on the surface, and after only a moment's hesitation she followed, dragging a deep breath into her
lungs and propelling herself down, eyes wide open
and gazing in wonder as instantly the reef came into
view. Still, after all the times Mia had seen it, it never
ceased to amaze her that beneath the tranquil azure
water lay a world of its own, gently swaying, colours
more magnificent, brighter, vibrant somehow, fishes
darting, pursed lips that looked rouged, gaping open
and closed, some so bold, so fearless she could touch
them, feel the smooth flesh glide through her hands,
tiny yellow fish dancing, darting around her like fairy
dust.

He watched, his greater lung capacity allowing him
to stay that dangerous moment longer, allowing him
to watch her rise to the surface from beneath, more
beautiful than any ocean creature, blonde curls
straightened by the force of the water now, a golden
stream that trailed behind her, breasts barely covered
by the tiny red triangles, the gorgeous swell of her
stomach. Her bronzed legs seemed to go on for ever,
parting as she did a vertical breast-stroke, allowing a
teasing glimpse of the hollows of her upper thighs,

and Ethan felt his groin kindle with lust, imagining the sweet, secret place within, a place he'd visited, a place he longed, needed, wanted, to return to.

He gulped air into his lungs as he hit the surface. His breathlessness had nothing to do with swimming and everything to do with the smiling face waiting for him, eyes as green as the water, her hair trailing along the surface. She looked like some mystical mermaid, some divine creature, and he ached, literally ached, to wrap his legs around her, to pull away the tiny red bikini bottom and claim her, his erection so fierce, his wanting so deep, it physically hurt to hold back. The feel of her hand on his shoulder was blistering in its effect, the top of her breasts rising and falling as she caught her own breath, the creamy flesh, usually covered by a T-shirt, already pinking up from the harsh Australian sun, tiny freckles appearing on her golden arms.

'Ready to go again?'

He wasn't.

All Ethan wanted to do was stay, to relish this moment for a little while longer, to hold this slice of time and somehow save it for later, remember the beauty on the surface, and ignore the irrefutable truth that lay beneath the innocence of her eyes, the vivid green with golden flecks, the arch of her eyebrows, her spiky eyelashes. The lush curve of her mouth was so moist, so tempting he wanted to drink from it. The sun glistened on her skin, and her almost childlike smile was such a contrast to the voluptuous woman beneath the glass-like water, her body so overtly feminine, ripe with another man's child, his brother's child—and—he could live with that. He felt a closeness to the baby that defied his own harsh beliefs, already an immeasurable love for someone he had never met, for a child he couldn't wait to hold, but that Richard had been there, had touched her, held her, loved her—

Could he live with that too?

His indecision truly terrified him, from utter abhorrence, to outright rejection at first, but now, slowly, he was coming around to the idea. The lines he had drawn so fiercely in the sands of time between them were fading with each glimpse of a life beside her, rules he had imposed on himself paling into insignificance as he contemplated a future without her.

He didn't *understand*.

Didn't want to understand how she could want them both. And she did want him, Ethan knew that. The kiss in the shower had only confirmed what he knew. The heat, the sexual heat that radiated between them was so strong he could taste it, could reach out now into the charged air between them and grab hold of it, feel it in the palm of the hand he clenched beneath the surface. He didn't *understand* how she could be so ready to move on, her grief for her baby's father, for her lover, so, so *inadequate* somehow. Oh, she missed Richard. He'd heard her cry at night, after all, seen her eyes mist over, felt her mind wander when Richard had been mentioned or a song, a line in a film had somehow hit its mark. He didn't doubt she missed him, but the Mia he knew, the Mia he loved, should be on her knees.

On her knees as he would be if it were his love, if it were Mia ripped from him, taken from his life, his future, his dreams. He'd be on his knees, howling at the injustice, raw with agony, tortured with regret at the missing years.

He simply didn't understand.

She slipped away then, darting beneath him, slipping out of his grasp, barely a ripple on the surface to mark her exit, and he glimpsed then what Mia had felt seven years ago, when he had cut her out of his life, left her bereft, questions unanswered, all alone with nothing to cling to.

CHAPTER EIGHT

'I WANT to paint.'

They were barely inside the front door. A trail of sand on the cool marble tiles followed her as Mia headed purposely towards the alfresco area, not even bothering to turn on the lights as she went, her head full, bursting, with ideas, with colour, with passion, finally ready and not a moment too soon.

'Now?' She heard the incredulity in Ethan's voice. 'Mia, it's eleven at night; we've been out since seven. Surely you should rest, get some sleep…'

'I couldn't sleep.' An impatient shake of her head left him none the wiser. 'Ethan, I feel as if I've been asleep for weeks. You were right; I needed to get out there, to see it again, to hear the people's excitement as they witnessed the reef's beauty for the first time. This has been the best day…'

It had been. From the splendour of the reef, to the virgin beach where they had picnicked, every moment had been an awakening and it was far from over. Her skin still tingled from the sun's scorching kiss, like a shell to her ear she could still hear the ocean, see the vivid colours Ethan had taken her to in her mind's eye, and Mia knew she had to get it down now. 'Finally everything's come together; it's all here!' She tapped the side of her head, but Ethan shook his.

'And it will all still be there in the morning, Mia...'
he started, but she wasn't listening, pulling a dust
sheet from her canvas, pulling up a stool and staring
at the same work she'd stared at for weeks now, only
this time it was different. There was a fire in her eyes,
a purpose in her movements that had been missing
till now.

'Mia!' Ethan tried again, sensing her impatience at
the distraction he was causing. 'You can do all this
tomorrow.'

'It might not be *there* tomorrow.' Her eyes pleaded
with him to understand, to be quiet. 'Ethan, it isn't a
desk I can leave and come back to; it isn't a pile of
figures that might look clearer in the morning. With
what I do, there might be nothing left in the morning.
I have to take it while it's there, have to...' She trailed
off, realizing it was hopeless, that the austere busi-
nessman who stared back at her could never begin to
understand, but when he gave a tight nod, when he
headed to the kitchen and poured them both a long
drink, handing Mia's to her without a single word,
her smile contracted in disbelief for a second, grateful
eyes acknowledging his silence as finally *it* flowed,
as finally what she felt, the visions that had lurked in
the background for so long, sprang forth.

And even if Ethan didn't understand it, he had to
respect it, because watching her work, watching her
brush stroke the canvas, seeing her creation grow before his eyes, witnessing her talent, he could do nothing else.

On she worked, each stroke moving the image

closer to what they had witnessed that day, capturing the beauty the way no photo ever could, the depth of her imagination, the attention to detail, the sheer skill in those lithe fingers almost enough to hold his attention.

Almost.

The sheen of her skin as the sultry heat took effect, her arms lifting, gliding off her T-shirt in one lithe motion, and impatiently tossing it to the floor as on she worked. Her spinal column teasing him as she leant forward, his eyes following its trail, the red triangle of her bikini not enough to cover the peach of her buttocks, which rose occasionally out of the stool as she leant forward or shifted position, each tiny motion stirring him further.

'I'm going for a shower.'

She didn't even answer.

Didn't seem to notice him leave.

Didn't look up when, after the longest time, he returned.

'You're crying?'

'Happy tears.' Two glittering jewels flashed at him momentarily, blinding him with their beauty. 'I'm finally finished.' She turned back to her work and he walked up behind her, staring at the canvas but not even seeing it, his head so full it felt as if it might burst. For a slice of time he maybe even understood, knew how it must feel to act on impulse, to know, just know that the magic, the closeness, the beauty that was now mightn't be there in the morning, to understand that if he walked away now he might never come back, might never capture this moment again.

And he wanted this moment with her.

Knew with absolute clarity that what he was feeling was right.

Sure, he could weigh up the pros and cons, listen to his factual mind that always seemed louder than his heart, think of a million reasons why it could never work, but not one of them held a candle to how he felt standing there behind her now.

And as surely as Mia could hear the ocean in an imaginary shell he heard her voice then.

Maybe it's time to chase your own dreams, Ethan…

She *was* a dream, his dream, the nightly visitor to his subconscious, who invaded every inch of his personal space by her mere presence, and he could deny it no longer.

He *could* do this; could love her without question; *would* love her if she let him.

Would push aside the reservations that had held him back, quite simply because he could do nothing else.

Dragging a stool closer, he rested a hand on her shoulder as he sat behind her, both gazing at the underwater view she had created, living again the sensual beat they had danced to when they had left the world behind, the freedom they had found this very morning. He could feel the rapid rise and fall of her chest as she gasped tiny, shallow breaths. The tension that had simmered was rising to a crescendo now, bubbles of lust rising to the surface as her skin seemed to merge in with his, an extension of his own. Her long slender neck, the flickering pulse in its hollow, seemed to call his lips of its own accord. He felt it under his swollen mouth, capturing the beat with his tongue, the scent of her hair as it trailed across his cheeks, and he closed his eyes in regret, for all he had thrown away, for the conclusions he had drawn, for having doubted her, for not having been able to fully believe in the magic he had found that night.

As if on autopilot his hand slid down inside the flimsy fabric, no caution now, no turning back, purpose in his action, because it was now or never. He could feel her nipple beneath his fingers, the thud of her heart behind her breastbone as he gently rolled her nipple between the pads of his thumb and finger and pressed his torso against the spinal column that had teased him. And she arched backwards, the hollow of her neck the refuge for his free hand, locating her galloping pulse, leaning over her and soothing it with his cool lips.

'I can't, Ethan.' Her voice was a hoarse whisper, regret lacing every word. 'Can't do this; can't risk waking up in the morning and seeing regret…'

'There will be no regret, Mia. Not any more. I've lived with regret for seven years now and I'm not going to lose you twice. I'm not going to let my pride get in the way of us again. I can't go on like this, can't live a moment in this house and not have you. All of you.'

'Are you sure?' Her hand reached for his, stopping

its stealthlike movements, but the heat of his palm scorched into her breast, and she struggled internally, desperate to give in, to go with the feelings he instigated, for Ethan to blot out the loneliness, the agony, the tension that saturated every pore. Yet she was wired with vulnerability, terrified to feel again, to let him in only to have him walk away, couldn't survive the torture of a second rejection. 'Are you sure that you can forgive the fact it's Richard's baby…?'

'It has nothing to do with forgiveness,' Ethan said, his voice thick with emotion. 'I know that now, Mia. It's to do with acceptance. I didn't know if I could accept it at first, wasn't sure I could accept the fact that you and Richard…' He paused for a heartbeat, sensibility gushing in, and he blocked it, almost physically pushed the taunting questions away, such was his need, his want, his love. 'From the day I asked you to move in here, from the moment I saw you again, I've wanted you, Mia, wanted all of you; you know that as well as I do. But wanting is one thing, seeing it through is another. I can't just have you in my home as much as I can't just have you in my bed. That's why I've waited; that's why I've pushed you away. It *has* to be all of you, Mia.'

'And it has to be all of *you*, Ethan.' Her voice trembled as she recalled his rejection, the futile end to something so beautiful, the wasted years he had ripped away from them. 'You have to promise to talk to me, Ethan, to tell me what you're thinking, how you're feeling.'

'I will.'

'You have to!' There was urgency in her voice. 'You didn't even give me a chance to defend myself, threw away seven years that we could have spent together because you were too mistrusting to even contemplate there might be another side to the story, that Richard might not be telling the truth, too damned proud to ask me my truth.'

'I know that now.'

And such was the sincerity in his voice, such was the regret, the pain, the love behind his words it was enough to quell her fears, to finally admit that maybe they could make it after all. She nodded her understanding, closed her eyes as she moved her hand that had been stilling him away, leant back into him as his hand slid between her cleavage, fingers splaying between the two trembling mounds, the soft sheen of her skin like an accelerant as his fingers massaged her deeper.

'It will still be there in the morning,' he whispered, and this time she believed him, this time she understood that he knew what he was saying. Her neck arched further backwards, a strangled gasp in her throat as his hands inched down, leaving her exposed breast to the mercy of his lips as he leant over behind her, his jaw scratching the soft skin, his tongue working the taut nipples, teasing them ever longer, his thighs wrapped around hers, his hand massaging her stomach. And this time his touch wasn't cautious. This time she could feel the love, the passion, the reverence in his movements, holding the child within her in an almost proprietary gesture, cradling the swell of her stomach in his hands. She felt as if he had reached in and captured her soul, knew that his touch was more than just lust, more than just want, but about need and acceptance as well. That in touching her now he was taking all of her, and she surrendered to him then, kissed the last grey shadows of doubt goodbye, Ethan's touch all she needed to move on. His lips were moving upward now, kissing her ears, his hot breath driving her into a frenzy as her head spun, a dizzy frenzy of lust as a hand moved down, slipped into the bottom of her bikini. Probing fingers brushed the soft down as his other hand moved under her buttocks, coming at her from both directions, an onslaught of sensations she didn't know how to respond to, a driving need to turn around to face him, coupled with a selfish need to stay, to allow his skilful hands to work their magic, to carry on this teasing stroke, sliding into her warmth. A tiny groan escaped her lips but was drowned out in an instant by a shuddering gasp as his other hand captured the core of her womanhood, her buttocks rising out of the stool of their own accord, her back arching in delicious submission, legs twitching almost spasmodically as he brought her so damned close it was indecent.

'Ethan.' It was all she could manage, the single word a gasp, but he understood what she was saying, understood the language her body was speaking, freeing her for a second. As she turned around they faced each other head-on, perhaps for the first time. And he held onto her, guided her down as she lowered herself onto him, slid over his length, his arms steadying her as her head threw back, moving her, lifting her up and down his heated length as his face drowned in her bosom, feeling her thighs tighten around his back, her stomach swollen against his. He tried to hold back, terrified of hurting her, but she wouldn't let him, bucking against him, giving him the permission he needed to grind himself into her, to give into the spasm that racked his body, feeling her most intimate vice tightening convulsively around him. He let go then, shuddering into her, a primal groan escaping his lips as she dragged every last sweet drop out of him.

Exhausted but elated, she rested against him, lay her glowing cheeks on his damp shoulder, felt arms that would never let her fall wrap around her as her breathing caught up, as a heart that was beating wildly out of control finally tripped back into rhythm. And Mia knew then in a blinding flash of clarity that she could finally tell him the truth, because she wouldn't be shouting it in defence, but telling him for all the right reasons.

That Richard would understand.

'Ethan, about Richard…'

'Don't.' He lifted her back slightly, stared at her for the longest time. 'Not now, Mia, not when we've just found each other again. We've got the rest of our lives to sort things out. Like I said before, it will all still be there in the morning.'

CHAPTER NINE

IT WAS.

For seven years Mia had loved Ethan, had missed the beauty of waking beside him. Of feeling him curved into her back, his knees tucked behind hers, her head resting on his upper arm as his hand cupped her breast, while the other hand rested on her stomach, as if even in sleep he couldn't bear to let her go. Wriggling free, ignoring his low moan of protest, she turned to face him, scarcely able to believe that in all this time she'd never witnessed him relaxed, never known the ethereal beauty of his face without the stern mask he wore. She stared, capturing every feature, tracking with her artistic eyes the superb sculpture of his cheekbones, the strong jaw that looked softer in sleep, the dusting of an early-morning shadow that made her breasts tingle at the memory of its scratching feel against her skin. Her eyes worked lower, utterly uninhibited in the absence of his brooding gaze and she caught her breath in wonder. The morning sun rising through the unclosed shutters cast shadows on the hollows of his ribs, drew her eyes to his nipples dark as mahogany, a snaky ebony trail of hair guiding her downwards. She ached to pull the sheet away, and, she realized with a deep satisfaction, finally she could.

She was in bed beside the man she loved.

Finally, after so much want, so much need, so much pain, she could act on her impulses without reprimand, look into his eyes without fear of revealing the depth of her passion, because he felt it too.

Her hand crept boldly down, pushing away the crumpled cotton, and she stared at the tumid beauty, rising gently just at her will, as if her gaze, her need, was enough to rouse it. She couldn't not reach out and touch it, needed to feel its silken beauty in her hands, running a finger along its heated length, mentally pinching herself that it was hers to stroke, to hold, that it was her touch he responded to, and that knowledge made her bold. His eyes as they slowly opened made her feel so wanted, so adored, they made her feel safe.

'Good morning.' The two words were a low rumble, thick with desire and lust, no shadows of regret in the dark pools of his eyes, no hesitation in the hands that pulled her in closer, that parted her thighs as he softly slipped inside. And there was a tenderness to their lovemaking that hadn't been so visible before. Deep, slower strokes, the abandonment and furious possession of before replaced instead with the heady knowledge that time was on their side; that this was theirs to keep. And they stared at each other as they moved together, no words needed as their bodies spoke volumes, the intensity of their orgasms so overwhelming, shuddering through her, her hands clinging onto his back, dragging into his skin, his name escaping her lips. When tears filled her eyes she didn't blink them back, just let them fall, the release of emotion so intense, so cathartic it felt like a new awakening; that he was still there, still holding her, still loving her was like the sun coming up all over again.

'What are you doing today?'

She revelled in his question, revelled in the motion of another step forward.

'I've got the doctor's at nine. What about you?'

'I've got a video conference with the manager of the Sydney resort at nine-thirty and a solicitor's appointment at eleven.'

'Sorry.'

'For what?'

'Keeping you from work. I know you're in limbo…'

'And loving it.' He smiled. 'Heavens, Mia, I've worked eighty-hour weeks for as long as I can remember. I deserve this time away from the office. Anyway, when I arranged to work from *home* I was always planning that it would be for longer. None of us really knew Richard was going to die so soon, to go so quickly at the end…' His voice trailed off, Richard's memory hanging in the air between them, and the certainty that had gripped her last night intensified now. Mia knew without doubt that she had to tell him the truth, break the vow she had taken with Richard, but for all the right reasons; honesty was needed now if they were truly to move on. She would demand it from Ethan, and he had every right to demand it from her.

'There's something I need to tell you, Ethan,' she

said softly. Honesty a mere breath away, she swallowed hard, utterly unprepared in her speech, the truth something she hadn't even contemplated telling. 'Something you really need to know.'

'About?' His eyes narrowed, his hand idly stroking her stomach. He smiled occasionally as a foot or elbow hit its mark.

'About the baby, about Richard and I...'

His hand jerked away from her stomach, the shutters coming down on his eyes, and mentally she slammed her fingers in between, desperate to have her say, but Ethan got there first.

'Please, Mia.' Sitting up, he raked a hand through his unruly hair, shook his head as if clearing away an image. 'I can't go there. I know this is Richard's baby, I understand all that, accept it even, but I'm just not ready to...'

She glanced at the bedside clock, already nudging its way past eight, and she knew now wasn't the time, that what she had to say would affect them both, that it needed to be delivered with more subtlety than this busy morning allowed. 'This evening, then. Can we talk this evening?' When he didn't respond she pushed harder. 'Ethan there's something you need to know, something I need to share with you; now isn't the time for secrets.'

He gave a tiny nod, and she saw a flash in his eyes that looked almost like fear.

'We'll talk this evening,' she affirmed, slipping out of the bed and heading for the shower, the needles of water refreshing her. She was invigorated by the honesty that was just a mere few hours away, that finally after all this time there would be no lies between them, the thought of honesty more cleansing than the water that slid over her.

'I'd have liked to have been there today for you.' As she stepped out of the shower Ethan was standing waiting. 'I don't want you doing this alone.'

'I'm not alone.' Softly she kissed him, revelling a moment in his embrace. 'Not any more.'

It was probably for the best Ethan did have an appointment and couldn't accompany her. A niggling pain in her back that Garth had immediately picked up on had stretched her half-hour appointment to well past midday—strapped to monitors, being prodded and poked all to no apparent avail, and Garth's rather noncommittal response would have sent Ethan's calculating mind into a spin.

'Everything looks fine,' Garth concluded finally, staring at her rather extensive test results.

'I told you it was just a backache; surely it's way too soon to be labour?'

'Not really.' He gave a knowing smile. 'You're only five weeks away from your due date, Mia, and some babies like to make a grand entrance, but, like I said, everything looks fine on paper. Still, I'd be happier if you don't go wandering too far, okay? And now might be a good time to see about filling in all these forms? I've got a collection kit for the cord blood ready for when the baby comes, so apart from the forms all we have to do for now is take a blood sample today.'

Again, she thanked her lucky stars Ethan wasn't here now. Sitting in a doctor's surgery, however luxurious, certainly wasn't the place for him to find out her secret, and one glance at the paperwork Garth was pushing towards her would surely have revealed all to Ethan, or at the very least set his mind whirring into dangerous motion.

'You've done this before. Not the blood test, I mean, but the cord blood donation?' Mia checked for the hundredth time, and Garth nodded confidently.

'I have, though not as often as I'd like, I admit; unfortunately it doesn't enter most women's heads to donate the cord blood, which is a shame when it's such a simple procedure with such amazing potential. The main thing is to ensure it's stored correctly until it gets to one of the major centres.' He gave a sympathetic smile. 'I know this isn't what you had planned, I know from the little you've told me that you were hoping this procedure would save Richard's life, but if it all goes okay, Mia, this gift you're donating will save someone else's life, maybe a child…'

'Please, Garth.' His words, however well meant, weren't helping. Garth's words seemed to be leading to the very conclusion she and Richard had been so opposed to. And maybe because Mia knew tonight she was going to tell Ethan, she was able to finally open up a touch to her doctor. 'This was never just a *procedure* to Richard and me. This baby wasn't just a spare part, Garth; it wasn't just about providing a suitable donor for Richard. By the time we'd actually agreed and got the ball rolling I think we both knew it was going to be too late for Richard anyway, but it didn't matter.' Her hand clutched her stomach. 'I wanted this baby, Garth, and, even if it didn't save Richard, I'm proud that we did it, that Richard left a precious legacy. Even though he understood that for only a few precious days, he was so pleased, so proud…'

'And so should you be,' Garth said gently. 'Ethan too.' Seeing her agonized expression, he let out a sigh. 'You haven't told him any of this, have you?'

Mia shook her head.

'He loves you, Mia, he needs to know.' Startled eyes looked up and Garth gave a knowing nod. 'I'm not blind, Mia. You two were made for each other. Ethan can act as brittle and detached as he likes, but he loves you just as much as any doting father-to-be.'

Her hands massaged her temples, the tension of the lies that bound her finally catching up. 'Richard and I made a vow that we'd never reveal the reason I got pregnant, never reveal that the baby was conceived through artificial insemination. We didn't want the baby to even think it was borne from anything less than love.'

'Ethan needs to know, Mia.' Garth's voice was unequivocal. 'Some vows were made to be broken and this is one of them. This is good news, Mia,' Garth reiterated, and Mia nodded. 'Surely it can only make things easier for both of you? You have to tell him.'

'I will.' She nodded firmly. 'This evening. I'm going to tell him this evening.'

'Well, put some champagne in the fridge.' Garth smiled and as Mia opened her mouth to object he broke in. 'One glass.' He nodded. 'You deserve a celebration.'

CHAPTER TEN

RICHARD would understand.

Mia knew that now.

Richard would understand why she had to break the promise they'd made. And it wouldn't be hurled in defence, or said in regret; instead, God willing, it would draw Ethan closer, pave the way for a closer bond between him and the baby that would soon be a part of his life.

Garth's words had only served to clarify what she already knew.

Ethan needed to know.

A shiver of expectation ran through her as she let herself into the flat and laid her bulging bags on the table. Once tonight was over, finally they could move on...

Together.

No more lies, no more half-truths, just safe in the knowledge of their love for each other and the excitement of a future surely better shared.

Placing a bottle of champagne in the fridge, she decided she'd allow herself that one glass tonight, toast the delicious, precious future with Ethan. But there wasn't time to dwell, to indulge herself in daydreams. She wanted this to be perfect down to the very last detail, even the meal. Moreton Bay Bugs just as they'd shared their first meal together, and flowers, flowers everywhere.

Of course Ethan didn't possess a vase.

Or a candlestick!

But she made do with some paint jars of her own, melted wax into what she hoped weren't priceless saucers, her hands trembling with anticipation as she prepared the meal, laid the table, and finally the day that had dragged on for ever caught up with her. The clock marched forward, forcing her in and out of the shower with a yelp, hands so shaky she could barely put on her mascara, or do up the zip on her ice-white dress; she almost burnt herself trying to light the candles.

Ready.

Staring at her reflection, she swallowed back nerves as she heard the low purr of his sports car, fiddled with a stray blonde curl as she heard his impatient step on the staircase.

Ready to tell him what he deserved to know.

She stepped forward as she heard his key turn in the lock, one hand dusted to her stomach, the other to her throat, butterflies dancing in her body, anticipation in every cell, drenched in lust as the door pushed open. His beauty never failed to overwhelm her, his dark suit even on this humid night still impossibly uncrumpled, the only acknowledgement to the impossible heat a loosened tie around his thick throat. In the subdued lighting she couldn't read his expression, moving forward from the shadows, a nervous smile dancing on her lips, willing him to pull her into his arms, his touch all she needed to go on.

He didn't.

Like bandit screens shooting up at the bank, she felt the barriers between them before he even said a word, felt the bristling animosity emanating from him as she stepped blindly forward.

'Ethan?' The question in her voice needed an answer, she needed to hear him speak, for this horrible silence to end, for the man who had held her this morning to come back to her, but he stayed well away, walking into the lounge room, scathing eyes taking in the feminine, romantic scene as he tossed off his jacket, poured himself a shot of brandy and drank from the glass without even deigning her a glance.

'Ethan!' Her voice was more urgent now as she stepped towards him, determined to face this head-on, to find out what had caused his change in demeanor, to bridge the distance that again seemed to separate them. 'What's wrong?'

'You tell me, Mia.' His words were like pistol shots, the suspicious moody eyes horribly familiar as they stared back at her, the guarded man back where her lover had so recently stood. She opened her mouth to beg an explanation, to find out what on earth had happened to merit this change, but Ethan was too quick for her, filling the tiny, loaded silence with a question of his own. 'What was it you wanted to talk about tonight? You said you had something important to tell me.'

'I do.' She trembled, her mind darting in confusion, the speech she had prepared, the words she had chosen, useless now against the cold granite of his features. 'I did,' she corrected, her teeth chattering involuntarily, confusion ripping through her as everything suddenly shifted.

'Go on, then,' he said nastily, pouring himself another drink, then changing his mind, slamming the glass down onto the table so violently the contents spilled over, his anger simmering unexploded, and Mia knew she couldn't tell him like this. It was never supposed to be like this!

'It's difficult,' she started nervously. 'It's not something…'

'Not something you can just come out with?' Ethan broke in and she gave a hesitant nod. 'Then let me help you, Mia.' He was walking towards her, such utter malice in his eyes for a second she felt the cold fingers of fear clutching her heart.

'Ethan, please, you're scaring me!'

'Save the drama, Mia,' Ethan barked. 'You know I'd never hurt you.' He paused for the longest time, his breathing deep and ragged as her heart pounded in her ribcage up through her throat. She watched his face contort in fury before he finally spat out words with such contempt she reeled backwards. 'Do you know where I've been? Do you know why I'm so late?' He didn't wait for her answer. 'Because I've spent the day sitting in a solicitor's office, listening as to the reasons why Richard's house sale was taking so long, listening as to how Richard's ex-lover is disputing the will. That *he* feels the fact he lived there with Richard for five years and contributed to the mortgage and upkeep should mean that he merits a share of the proceeds.'

Narrow eyes gauged her reaction, that full mouth paling as she swallowed nervously; absolutely still, she stood, the only movement her earrings, quivering against her taut neck. 'You don't seem surprised.'

'I'm not.' Her voice was so hoarse, her throat so dry Mia had to clear it before she continued. 'I guess Michael has every right to feel he deserves—'

'So you know him?'

'Of course I know him. He was Richard's lover...' Anguished eyes met his. 'Ethan, I'm sorry you had to find out this way, sorry that I didn't have the courage to tell you about Richard before. He wanted you to know, wanted so much to tell you, but he just couldn't.'

'Why?' Black eyes glinted in the semi-darkness, his mouth like a taut crossbow. 'Did he think that I wouldn't understand?'

'You might have,' Mia begged. 'You probably would have,' she conceded, 'but, Ethan, your parents wouldn't have understood, never in a million years, and Richard didn't want to put you in an awkward situation. He told me how he tried to tell them once, how your father...' Her hands shot up to her face, the jigsaw tumbling down and falling into ugly place. 'That must have been when he said he slept with me. He said it was easier to lie, to tell them what they wanted to hear—that must have been what he meant.'

'He never slept with you, did he?'

'I already told you that, Ethan. Richard was making it up and now you know why…' Mia responded, but her voice trailed off as Ethan stepped closer, his face white in the candlelight, dark hollows under his eyes, every muscle clenched in suppressed rage, and she'd have rather he shouted, rather he unleashed his fury, because the hollow rage behind his whisper was far more unapproachable.

'He *never* slept with you,' Ethan said again, very slowly, very deliberately, taking in every flicker of her reaction, his eyes raking down to the swell of her stomach, screwing his eyes closed for a second as if the truth were more than he could bear. 'What were you going to tell me tonight, Mia? That you weren't a hundred per cent sure? That maybe it wasn't Richard's child after all, cover all bases just in case…'

'In case of what?'

'In case I found out later. In case I asked for a DNA work up or the baby got sick and I found out, found out that this wasn't nor ever could have been Richard's child. Slip it in now that there's a chance someone else could be the father to maybe safeguard you for later? Is that how your twisted mind works, Mia? Is that how you decided to trap me? By making love to me, by reeling me in until I'm so deep in love that I'll agree to anything, love any man's child as if it were my own, as if it had my own blood running through its veins…'

'You bastard…' White lips chattered around the

words, the cuss delivered with such force even Ethan looked shocked, Mia's eyes glittering with rage now, every fibre of her body trembling with the injustice of it all. 'You dare to stand here and say you'd never hurt me. Well, you're a liar, Ethan Carvelle, because again and again you hurt me, over and over you inflict pain and I don't deserve it…'

'You're the liar, Mia.' Walking over, he held her arms. 'He was gay, for God's sake, Mia, and you let me believe he was your lover, tried to pass this child off as his! You're the one inflicting pain…'

'No.' She attempted to wriggle away, but his grip was tight and it was Mia blind with fury now, Mia kicking up her foot to his shin, like a furious animal, to escape his grasp, and finally he gave in, loosened his grip and she stood there, tears streaming down her face as she stared back at this impossible stranger. 'You make it so hard to love you, Ethan. You make it so hard to be honest, to be open. You're so damn sure we're all waiting to get you, so damn sure the world is your enemy, when the truth is it's as good and as kind as you want it to be. I loved Richard, I wanted his baby, but I never slept with him, not even once, but this is his baby, Ethan—'

'Oh, please,' he roared. 'You're not making any sense.'

'I'm making perfect sense, Ethan. If you got off your high horse long enough to think things through rationally, you'd realize that you've answered your own question: this baby does have Carvelle blood running through its veins; it was Richard's only hope of survival! Work it out, Ethan; you're the one with the supposed brains! Your brother had cancer, for God's sake. All the family tests for a match came back as unsuitable, as you pointed out before. It's the twenty-first century; you don't have to sleep with someone to bear their child...' Blinded by tears, she turned away, ran into the bedroom and fumbled for the lock, ignoring his pounding on the door, her whole body racked with tears as he demanded to be let in.

'Mia, let me talk...'

'I'm through talking, Ethan, through defending myself to you.'

'I didn't know!' His voice was a desperate roar. 'When I heard Richard was gay, what the hell was I supposed to think?'

'You should have come to me.' Anguished gasps racked her body, a crippling pain ripping through where her soul used to be, forcing her to double up against the door as Ethan pounded away. 'You should have been able to talk to me first without jumping to your own appalling conclusions.'

'Mia, please!'

'No!' Her voice was definite. 'I'm not going to let you do this, Ethan. I can't live like this a moment longer, can't live my life waiting for the next onslaught, the next barrage of accusations. I just want you to go away.'

'Let me in, Mia.' The door was buckling under the weight of his shoulders, his voice a loud roar as he demanded she open it. 'Let me in.'

'I can't, Ethan. I can't let you in.' The agony in her voice reached him; she could almost feel him slump against the door. 'I can't keep letting you into my life just to have you hurt me again.'

'It won't be like that, now I know...'

'Now I've passed some imaginary test?' Mia responded. 'Now that I've provided you with a satisfactory answer? It's supposed to be innocent until proven guilty, Ethan, not the other way around. I was going to tell you about the baby tonight, because I thought it was something you deserved to know. Instead you jumped right in, assumed the worst from me all over again, dragged the truth out of me, took away my chance to explain the way I wanted to...'

So deep was her pain, so violent her tears, it took a moment to register that the knot in her stomach wasn't a stitch, the gulping agony of her tears. Her hand shot to her stomach, fingers pushing into the tense knot of muscle, her breath catching in her throat.

'Mia?' She could hear his voice, the angry demands of before gone now. 'Please, just let me in.'

She didn't answer, instead she stood in the darkness, willing the moments to pass, willing to exert some control on her body. But just as she thought it was fine, that surely she had been mistaken, the pain returned, more intense this time than before, causing her to double over, a strangled scream escaping her lips as the full realization of her situation hit.

'Mia?''

As if sensing something was wrong his voice softened, the knocking on the door more urgent than angry now.

'It's the baby.' Unlocking the door, she stood there, seeing his aghast, stricken face, the panic in his eyes.

'It can't be...' He raked a hand through his hair, screwed his eyes closed with regret. 'It's too soon.'

'It's now, Ethan.' She gasped, doubling over as another contraction took hold. 'Ring Garth, the hospital, get the car...'

For once he did as he was told, guiding her down the steps, holding her close as a contraction overwhelmed her, before gently easing her into the passenger seat, snapping into assertive mode, calm apparently unruffled, but she knew from the pounding muscle in his cheek as he barked orders into the speaker phone that it was all an act, that he was as scared and as terrified as her.

'This is my fault.' He glanced over, his knuckles white as he gripped the steering wheel. 'I shouldn't have said anything, shouldn't have confronted—'

'It's no one's fault.' Her toes were curling, each pain more intense than the last, her hand clinging onto the handle above the door in an effort to hold on. 'I had some backache, a few contractions this morning. Garth said there was a chance...'

'You never told me...'

She gave a hollow laugh.

'When did you give me the chance, Ethan?'

Oh, the bliss of the bright lights of the hospital, the sweet relief of making it as they screeched into the forecourt, a team of staff waiting with a wheelchair, bundling her into knowing arms as Ethan raced around to the passenger side.

'I'll just move the car.' His hands reached out for hers. 'I'll be with you in a moment…'

'No!' Determined eyes met his, her hand shooting up, slowing the hive of activity. She was determined to regain a semblance of control as her treacherous body hurtled out of bounds. 'Go home, Ethan.'

'Go home?' She saw the dart of confusion in his eyes, heard the utter incredulity in his voice, but she was beyond comforting him, beyond trying to reason with him now. 'How the hell do you expect me to go home now?'

'Go home, Ethan.' Tears were streaming down her face, but it had nothing to do with the pain that shuddered her body and everything to do with the man who stood before her, the difficult, beautiful, complex man who over and over had spurned her love, who over and over had chosen to doubt her. 'I'll ring you when it's over.'

'I need to be with you, Mia.' The staff were moving on now, ushering her to the lift, and he raced behind, cramping himself between the closing doors and squeezing into the confined space. 'If we're ever going to make it then surely I should be there with you now, there beside you when you need me most.'

'But I don't need you, Ethan.' The doors slid open, the corridors blurring as they moved her along, the familiar face of Garth a welcome focal point as she entered the unfamiliar.

'We need to get her inside.' Garth's voice was

calm, his manner assured. 'It's better that you leave, Ethan.'

'Never.' Proudly he shook his head and she ached for him, ached for this strong, lonely man, suddenly trapped like a wounded animal.

'Can we have a moment alone, Garth?' Amazingly her voice was calm, in control even; her request met with a questioning look from Garth, answered with a brief nod from Mia. 'Just a moment, please.'

Alone she faced him, faced the man she loved, the man she wanted beside her now more than ever, but as hard as it was to ask him to leave, it was easier than letting him stay, glimpsing his dazzling love...

Until the next time.

'I love you, Ethan,' she said softly. 'I love you, I always have, but what you fail to understand is that I don't need you. I haven't been living my life waiting for you to come back to me, haven't spent my days scheming how to get you back, or how then to keep you. The simple truth is that I've lived my life how I wanted it to be, made decisions I fully intended to see through—alone.'

'But this morning...'

'This morning was perfect.' Her eyes clouded over at the memory, weakening for a tiny moment, then holding firm. 'This morning was how it could have been, but, Ethan, I'm not prepared to live like this. I deserve to be loved unreservedly—'

'You are.'

She shook her head. 'It's as if you're waiting to be proven right, Ethan. Waiting for me to show my true colours…' She swallowed hard. 'One day I'll make a mistake, one day I'll undoubtedly do something that I'm not proud of; what then, Ethan? Tonight I can justify my actions; tonight you're sorry for the pain because it's you who's wrong. What happens when it's my turn to make a mistake, Ethan? What will happen to your unreserved love then?'

'Mia, don't—'

'Please.' She held up a trembling hand, couldn't take the pain a moment longer, couldn't let him in again only to have him shut her out. 'If you really love me you'll go home, Ethan; you'll respect my wishes and walk away.'

'No.' He found his voice then, gripped her hand as another contraction tore through her, even signalled for a nurse to take her to the people she needed right now.

'I'll never walk away from you again, Mia, but I will give you space, if that's what you need.' She opened her mouth to protest, but he shook his head. 'I'll be here, Mia.' He gestured to the waiting room. 'I won't come in, won't make a sound, but if you change your mind, if you…' He didn't finish, just gave a proud nod as Garth stepped out, took the handles of the chair and wheeled her away.

CHAPTER ELEVEN

ETHAN felt it too.

Every tortured, agonized, scream ripped through him, compounded his own pain, and rammed home what he had again thrown away, all that he had lost. He ached to go to Mia, needed to be in there, holding her, helping her, being there, but he didn't.

And for once it wasn't pride that held him back, but respect.

Wasn't his ego that stopped him from stalking through the delivery doors and demanding inclusion—but humility that forced him out.

Pacing the tiny room, he felt he might explode, pathetic excuses for his behaviour springing to mind, and he tossed them all out, knowing it was too little, too late. Sinking into a chair, he rested his hands on his head, surveyed with painful honesty the devastation he alone had caused—as trusting as a child she had forgiven him, loved him all over again and how had he repaid her?

Black rivers of bile swirled in his stomach, fist clenched against his temples, each gut-wrenching scream emanating from the birthing suite lacerating him deeper, twisting the knife wound he had inflicted on himself.

'Ethan?' The tiny whimper had his head jerking up,

eyes snapping open, every nerve taut; sure, sure he must be mistaken.

'Ethan?' This time he knew he hadn't misheard, this time her shout echoed down the hallway, forcing him to his feet, spinning on the spot for a futile moment, torn, literally torn with indecision. His first instinct was to race to her side, to be there with her, for her, but he held back, trying to do the right thing, to do the one thing he hadn't been able to manage till now—to give her the benefit of the doubt.

'I think you're wanted.' Garth's face was at the door, but it wasn't friendly.

'I thought she might be cursing me...' He ran a shaking hand over his chin, took a few steadying breaths before nodding to the doctor. 'Can I go in?'

'For now.' Garth caught his sleeve as he darted out of the waiting room, fixed Ethan with a firm glare. 'But if she asks you to leave, you go.' His voice was firm and Ethan nodded, but Garth hadn't quite finished. 'And if I ask you to leave, the same thing goes; she doesn't need her mind messed with right now.'

He nearly agreed, such was his devastation he almost meekly complied, but his humility was reserved for Mia, *her* acceptance all he needed. His back might be against the wall, but he'd go down fighting.

'I'll leave only if Mia asks.' As Garth opened his mouth to argue Ethan got there first, eyeing the doctor's T-shirt and jeans with distaste. 'Shouldn't you be in theatre gear or something? Shouldn't you have a mask?'

'This is a natural birthing suite,' Garth responded

tartly. 'Our policy is to make the environment as homely as possible for the ladies, to keep hospital attire and equipment to the minimum.'

'God!' Ethan whistled. 'Is this the hippy mumbo-jumbo I'm paying for? What if something goes wrong?'

'Birthing is a natural process.'

He didn't have time for this, didn't have time to stand and argue, not when she was calling for him.

'Look, Garth, just do your job.' Ethan bristled. 'I'm the one paying your over-inflated bill, remember?'

He stalked into the room, where it took his eyes a moment to adjust to the semi-darkness, the overwhelming scent of incense filling his nostrils, the bizarre sound of birds chirping filling his ears and two man-hating midwives staring at him suspiciously as he stood there, clearly overdressed in his formal suit, watching as they massaged Mia's back, stroked the hair back from her drenched forehead, comforted her in a way he felt only he should be able to do.

'She's in pain.' Ethan's eyes swung to the doctor as he entered behind him, a guttural groan escaping Mia's lips as she screwed her eyes closed and gritted her teeth.

'She's doing wonderfully,' Garth said, his patronizing tone the very last thing Ethan needed right now.

'Give her something...' Ethan insisted, but it was Mia who answered.

'I want this to be natural,' she gasped.

'Sod natural.' He raked a hand through his hair, berating himself all over again; all the things he had wanted to say, all the things he had promised he'd do if only she called him, seemed to have fled from his mind. He'd never felt more scared, more out of control in his life! Everyone in the room seemed to know what they were doing; every one had a place in this except him. 'You're in pain.'

'Oh, this isn't pain.' Her eyes met his then, eyes that seemed dull now, eyes that told the tale of all he had put her through. 'This is nothing compared to what you did to me.'

'I know.'

For ever the silence dragged on. He wanted them all to go, to leave, to say all he had in private, but no one seemed to be going anywhere.

'I'm sorry,' he said finally, knowing how lame his words sounded, swearing internally to make it all up to her just as soon as this was over, just as soon as they were alone, but Mia, it seemed, had other ideas.

'If I let you stay, Ethan, if I let you be a part of this...' She straightened up then, the agony over till the next time, nodding to the midwife to let her go, pulling her massive oversize T-shirt further down her thighs in a bizarre attempt to make sure she was decent. 'Seven years ago you walked away from me without a backwards glance, never gave me another thought—' she started, but Ethan shook his head, stopping her at the first hurdle.

'I thought about you every day.'

'Liar,' Mia snarled.

'No...' Reaching in his jacket, he pulled out his wallet, snapping it open and holding it under her face, watching every flicker of her reaction as she stared at the photo. There they were, in a photo taken at the restaurant on their first meeting. Younger, happier, so, so much more carefree than they were now, tears filling her eyes as she stared at the face that had fuelled her dreams all those long, lonely nights, the face she had glimpsed that one magical time when the world had been good and kind.

'When did you get this?'

'On my way back to Sydney?' His voice was tentative, unsure of her reception. 'You've been next to my heart since then, Mia.'

'So why…?' Her voice trailing off, she doubled over as pain took hold and as the midwives stepped forward, as she leant again on them, Ethan bit back a curse, held it in till she could speak again, resisted the urge to push them away, to clear the room and just be with her.

'What the hell is that?' He bristled as an annoying chirrup filled the room, snapping a finger on the off button of the CD player, the one thing in the room he knew how to operate.

'It's the relaxing sounds of a rainforest.' The midwife shot him a look.

'Torture in the rainforest, more like,' Ethan murmured.

'It helps me to focus,' Mia gasped, but Ethan shook his head, walking over, and such was his presence, such was the purpose in his movement, even the proprietary midwives stepped back. Taking her arms, he steadied her, held on to her till the contraction finally subsided.

'Focus on this,' he said softly, staring right at her, not blinking, not moving, just holding her with his eyes.

And suddenly it was just the two of them, the world melting into the background, a temporary reprieve from her pain as she listened, watched that delicious mouth move, heard the occasional falter in his voice as finally he delivered his truth.

'You're right, Mia: all along I've been waiting for you to prove me right, waiting for you to somehow slip off the pedestal I put you on, and you ask why. Why couldn't I believe you? Why didn't I think love could be that simple? Because...' a beat of a pause stilled him, and she saw the aching chasm of despair in his eyes, almost reached out to halt him, to stop him reducing himself to the awful truth, but she needed to hear it to understand it, and perhaps, more poignantly, knew Ethan needed to voice it too '...I'd never known love. Never had it, never felt it and I never missed it either, couldn't miss what I didn't know.' His words were delivered without a trace of self pity, but they were steeped in painful truth. 'And then you came along, the prettiest, sweetest thing I'd ever seen in my life, stepped into my world and straight into my heart as if I'd surely spent my whole life waiting, and I couldn't believe it was that easy, couldn't believe that was all there is to it—that you fell in love and lived happily ever after.'

Tears were streaming down her face, angry ones,

but not at him, but for all he'd been through, for the lonely nights of his childhood, for the shallow love of a cheque-book, and there was pride in her eyes too that this difficult, brooding man could somehow admit the truth, could, in front of this most hostile audience, lay open his heart and share his pain.

'I should have told you sooner, but Richard and I...' She started, words trailing off as her body took over. 'You have to let me in, Ethan, have to come to *me* with what you're feeling, what you're thinking, run things by me before racing off to your own conclusion.'

'I know.'

She thought she could do it, thought she had it all in order, but just when she gained a semblance of control, just when she thought an end was in sight, the ground shifted again, her whole epicentre shifting, filled with a desperate need to push, an urgent primal need engulfing her, yet making her strong, propelling her into action, the hands of time forcing a decision, because if he stayed now, if he shared in this precious, imminent moment then the ties that bound them would be too tight to ever leave.

'So tell me.' Her tiny jaw was set in grim determination, her face a glistening pink sheen as she stared defiantly at him.

'Tell you what?'

'What you're thinking, what you're feeling. I need to know, Ethan.'

'That I love you.' Perplexed, he stared at her as she shook her head angrily, her hands clutching her stomach. 'That next time something happens I'll ask you—'

'Not good enough, Ethan. I need to know what's in here.' Her hand thumped his chest, her eyes imploring him to understand. 'I need to know how you're feeling. I can't live with your capricious moods, can't keep trying to second-guess what's going on in that closed mind of yours. I need you to let me in...'

He didn't know what she wanted, couldn't fathom what she needed, his mouth opening and closing, his mind racing to find the words that were needed. Then like a swirling fog lifting he understood, understood that his doubts were okay, that he could voice them, say them, share them.

'I want to bring up the baby as mine.' That stiff upper lip trembled as her eyes finally met his. 'I want to be like a father to it, but I still want him to know the truth, want him to know about his real—'

'It might be a she,' Mia corrected.

'*She* sounds just as good,' Ethan responded quickly. 'I just want to be there beside you, somehow make up for all the time we lost, all the time I made us...'

'And?' There was nothing soft about her voice, a snapped command as need took over, as a baby that really needed to be born decided it had waited long enough. 'Isn't there something else you should be saying at this point, Ethan? Isn't there something I might really need to hear right now?'

He gave a perplexed shake of his head, glancing at

the midwife for inspiration, then doing a double take, appalled that a nose ring was considered suitable attire in such a reverend setting!

'I think Mia needs a little incentive right now, Ethan,' Garth nudged. 'Perhaps now might be a good time to say what she really wants to hear, what she really needs to help her through this turbulent time.'

'Oh, that…' A tiny smile inched across his face as the midwives glared back expectantly, then he stepped in and took over, his strong arms holding her up as she bore down, superior, scathing but infinitely loving as he pulled her in closer and softly whispered into her ear, his touch, his embrace, his mere presence everything she needed right now.

The only man in the whole world who could suffice.

Wrapping her in his loving arms, holding her close as she faced the most tumultuous journey of her life; the only man who could make her smile, laugh even, at the most overwhelming moment in her life.

'Hurry up, darling; I've got a bottle of champagne on ice.'

CHAPTER TWELVE

HOLDING the precious parcel, staring at the pretty rosebud mouth opening in protest, defiant blue eyes already tinged with green flecks staring angrily back at him, her little fists clenched in rage as she demanded yet another feed, Ethan felt his heart spill over.

What wasn't there to love?

Holding her arms out, Mia took the angry bundle, smiling down in utter wonder as she nursed her child, scarcely able to comprehend she was finally, after all this time, really here. As she looked up her breath caught in her throat, her head tightening in disbelief as she stared back at Ethan.

He was really here too.

More exhausted than she'd ever seen him, dark smudges under his eyes, his suit for once crumpled and his expensive silk tie undoubtedly lost for ever, but he was here, and, from the love blazing in his eyes as he stared back at her, it was for good this time.

'She's got Richard's hair.' His strong fingers stroked the Titian locks, his Adam's apple bobbing up and down as his face quilted with emotion.

'You were wrong, what you said in the delivery room.' Mia's voice was soft, her eyes gazing at the babe in her arms, the world put to rights as peace finally took hold. 'You were loved all along, you know; Richard really did love you.'

'Did you ever tell him?' Ethan's voice was thick. 'About us, about that night?'

She gave a tiny nod. 'A few weeks after it happened,' she admitted. 'My dad had lost his job and everything seemed such a mess, and I suppose he was there for me. I really needed to confide in someone— not that it helped.' She gave a soft laugh. 'I can see now why the whole thing made Richard so uncomfortable. I thought at the time it was because you were his brother, but I guess, looking back, he was riddled with guilt for inadvertently breaking us up. Maybe that's why he stayed away from you,' she said softly. 'Maybe that's why he couldn't face you, because he knew deep down how much he'd hurt you, how much he'd hurt us both.'

'It must have been hard for him,' Ethan murmured, 'carrying that secret all these years.'

'Perhaps this was his way.' Her fingers traced the soft apple of her baby's cheek. 'Somewhere, deep down, maybe he knew that a baby would bring us together, that sooner or later you'd find out that she was his and…'

Ethan gave a slow nod, the possibilities endless, the truth too hard to fathom sometimes, but, staring at the innocent face, he knew it was meant to be, that the gift of love was sometimes just too big to comprehend; but it *was* a gift and one he intended to cherish.

'Should you ring your parents?' Her voice was apprehensive; she was scared to let the world in just yet but knew she had to. 'Shouldn't you let them know that they're grandparents?'

'Good God, no!' He gave her a slightly appalled look. 'I'm not ringing them twice in one day.'

'Twice?'

He pulled his diary out of his pocket and tossed it on the bed. 'Pick a day and then I'll call them—kill two birds with one stone.'

'Pick a day?'

'For the wedding.'

A deep blush whooshed up her cheeks. 'Ethan, you don't have to marry me. What I said in there...'

'You meant,' Ethan quipped. 'Now, had you chosen a rather less barbaric way to give birth—' for the hundredth time he pulled up his shirt sleeve, almost proudly displayed the nail marks on his forearm as Mia slunk back into her pillow '—then you could blame it on the drugs, but, given this was an entirely natural labour, I don't think you've got an excuse. In fact if I remember correctly—'

'Don't.' Her hand came up to her scorching cheeks; she was mortified at her own presumption in the birthing suite. 'Please don't remind me; it was awful...'

'It was perfect.' His face softened into a smile. 'So all you have to do now is pick a day. I've already chosen the location.'

'Oh, you have, have you? I thought we were going to discuss things from now on, talk...'

'So there's no room for romance, then?' An eyebrow shot up. 'No room for surprises?'

'Okay,' she grumbled, 'so where's this fabulous, romantic location you've chosen?'

'Our rainforest.' Ethan smiled. 'Our rainforest where we're going to build our own extremely environmentally friendly hotel, build our own little patch of paradise; where we'll raise lots of happy, fat babies during the day and spend the nights making more; of course, if you can think of somewhere better, if you've got an idea…'

'No!' Her voice stopped his teasing tirade and something told him it was a time to be serious, a time to be still. 'I mean, I don't have a better idea, it sounds wonderful.' Her eyes held his as he came over and cradled the two precious females in his safe, strong arms.

'Have you thought of a name?'

Mia nodded.

'Hope.' Staring at Ethan, she tried to gauge his reaction, gave a tremulous smile as he softly repeated it.

'Hope.'

And this time he didn't stumble over it as he had back in the church, didn't falter on the concept as he had way back then—that difficult word made easy with love on their side.

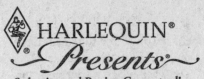

HARLEQUIN®
Presents

Seduction and Passion Guaranteed!

Legally wed, but he's never said...
"I love you."

They're...

Wedlocked!

**The series
in which
marriages are
made in haste...
and love
comes later...**

**Look out for more Wedlocked! marriage stories
in Harlequin Presents throughout 2005.**

Coming in May:
THE DISOBEDIENT BRIDE
by Helen Bianchin
#2463

Coming in June:
THE MORETTI MARRIAGE
by Catherine Spencer
#2474

www.eHarlequin.com

HPWL3

HARLEQUIN®
Presents®

Seduction and Passion Guaranteed!

He's got her firmly in his sights
and she's got only one chance of
survival—surrender to his
blackmail...and him...in his bed!

Bedded by... *Blackmail*

Forced to bed...then to wed?

**A new miniseries
from Harlequin Presents...**

Dare you read it?

Coming in May:
THE BLACKMAIL PREGNANCY
by *Melanie Milburne* #2468

www.eHarlequin.com   HPBBB2

If you enjoyed what you just read,
then we've got an offer you can't resist!

Take 2 bestselling love stories FREE!

Plus get a FREE surprise gift!

Clip this page and mail it to Harlequin Reader Service®

IN U.S.A.	IN CANADA
3010 Walden Ave.	P.O. Box 609
P.O. Box 1867	Fort Erie, Ontario
Buffalo, N.Y. 14240-1867	L2A 5X3

YES! Please send me 2 free Harlequin Presents® novels and my free surprise gift. After receiving them, if I don't wish to receive anymore, I can return the shipping statement marked cancel. If I don't cancel, I will receive 6 brand-new novels every month, before they're available in stores! In the U.S.A., bill me at the bargain price of $3.80 plus 25¢ shipping & handling per book and applicable sales tax, if any*. In Canada, bill me at the bargain price of $4.47 plus 25¢ shipping & handling per book and applicable taxes**. That's the complete price and a savings of at least 10% off the cover prices—what a great deal! I understand that accepting the 2 free books and gift places me under no obligation ever to buy any books. I can always return a shipment and cancel at any time. Even if I never buy another book from Harlequin, the 2 free books and gift are mine to keep forever.

106 HDN DZ7Y
306 HDN DZ7Z

Name	(PLEASE PRINT)	
Address	Apt.#	
City	State/Prov.	Zip/Postal Code

Not valid to current Harlequin Presents® subscribers.

Want to try two free books from another series?
Call 1-800-873-8635 or visit www.morefreebooks.com.

* Terms and prices subject to change without notice. Sales tax applicable in N.Y.
** Canadian residents will be charged applicable provincial taxes and GST.
   All orders subject to approval. Offer limited to one per household.
   ® are registered trademarks owned and used by the trademark owner and or its licensee.

PRES04R   ©2004 Harlequin Enterprises Limited

eHARLEQUIN.com

The Ultimate Destination for Women's Fiction

Becoming an eHarlequin.com member is easy, fun and **FREE!** Join today to enjoy great benefits:

- **Super savings** on all our books, including members-only discounts and offers!

- Enjoy **exclusive online reads**—FREE!

- Info, tips and **expert advice** on writing your own romance novel.

- FREE romance **newsletters,** customized by you!

- Find out the latest on your **favorite authors.**

- Enter to win exciting **contests and promotions!**

- Chat with other members in our **community message boards!**

To become a member,
visit www.eHarlequin.com today!

INTMEMB04R

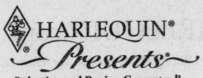

HARLEQUIN®
Presents
Seduction and Passion Guaranteed!

Introducing a brand-new trilogy by
Sharon Kendrick

THE
ROYAL HOUSE
OF
CACCIATORE

Passion, power & privilege – the dynasty continues
with these handsome princes...

Welcome to Mardivino—a beautiful and wealthy
Mediterranean island principality, with a prestigious
and glamorous royal family. There are three
Cacciatore princes—Nicolo, Guido and
the eldest, the heir, Gianferro.

Next month (May 05), meet Nico in
THE MEDITERRANEAN
PRINCE'S PASSION #2466

Coming in June: Guido's story, in
THE PRINCE'S LOVE-CHILD #2472

Coming soon: Gianferro's story in
THE FUTURE KING'S BRIDE

Only from Harlequin Presents

www.eHarlequin.com

HPRHC